# Veronica Knows Best

*Nancy K. Robinson*

**APPLE**
PAPERBACK

SCHOLASTIC INC.
New York Toronto London Auckland Sydney

ISBN 0-590-40510-1

12 11 10 9 8 7 6 5 4 3 2 1          1          9/8 0 1 2 3 4/9

Printed in the U.S.A.

*To Ed Shaw, Veronica's friend
and mine. . . .*

Other Apple Paperbacks
by NANCY K. ROBINSON

*Mom, You're Fired*
*Oh Honestly, Angela*
*Just Plain Cat*
*Wendy and the Bullies*
*Veronica the Show-Off*

Tripper & Sam #1
*The Phantom Film Crew*

Tripper & Sam #2
*Danger on the Sound Track*

Tripper & Sam #3
*The Ghost Who Wanted To Be a Star*

# The New Veronica

"Veronica has improved," Chris's mother said at breakfast. "She seems to be taking more of an interest in other people. I think she changed a lot over the summer."

"I'll bet," Chris muttered.

"No, it's true," his mother went on. "I bumped into her yesterday in the elevator. She asked all about you. She wanted to know if you'd had a nice summer."

"It's a trick," Chris said, and wondered why grown-ups always fell for that sort of thing. He was disappointed in his mother.

"Well, I told her that your cousin Julie had come to visit for a week and that you'd passed your intermediate swimmer's course at the YMCA. She said she thought your summer sounded very 'rich and rewarding.'"

Chris was startled. He would have expected Veronica to say something like, "You're kidding! Chris is only an intermediate? I got my advanced swimmer's card years ago."

Veronica lived in the same apartment building, right across the hall from Chris. Chris had always considered her a stuck-up snob and the biggest show-off he had ever come across.

But the new Veronica sounded even worse than the old one. Chris did not think that kids his own age had any business using words like "rich and rewarding."

"She's just trying to get attention," Chris said.

"Everyone needs attention," his mother said sadly. "Veronica probably needs it more than other children. I think she was expecting her father to invite her to visit him in California this summer, but she ended up visiting her grandfather in Vermont, instead."

Chris did not want to waste any energy thinking about Veronica. It was the first day of school and he was very excited. He was meeting his best friend Peter at the corner in ten minutes.

Peter had spent the summer with his parents on an island off the coast of Maine. And Chris had been waiting all summer for him to get back.

Peter appreciated a good joke more than anyone Chris knew. He was an expert on fine jokes, and Chris had a joke for Peter that he knew was the best joke he had ever heard.

Chris had been very careful with that joke. He had told his mother, and she had laughed so hard, she had started to cry. But he made her promise not to tell anyone else.

Chris had even timed the joke to make sure he could tell it easily in the five blocks it took them to walk to school. He did not want to feel rushed. He had walked those blocks the day before with his father's stopwatch, and was pleased to find there were two whole blocks for Peter to collapse with laughter and beg Chris to repeat the joke.

"This guy is driving along the highway. . . ."

Chris tried to put the joke out of his mind. He knew it was a bad idea to over rehearse.

"Poor Veronica," his mother was saying. "She must feel pretty lonely with no one around except her baby-sitter, that old Mrs. Moore. Her mother is still in Europe taking the latest 'youth cure' at some health resort in Switzerland. Veronica starts school today, too. That's early for a private school.

She asked me what time you were going to be leaving for school."

Suddenly Chris was alert. "You didn't tell her, did you?"

"Of course I did," his mother said.

"How could you?" Chris felt like shouting. "She'll want to walk with me to the corner."

"What's wrong with that?" his mother asked.

"If Peter sees me walking with Veronica, he'll walk ahead."

Chris knew it would take a whole block to catch up to Peter. It would spoil his timing. He decided to leave right away to avoid running into Veronica.

When he got to the front door of his apartment, he lay down on his stomach and put his eye right against the crack under the door.

He saw a shadow moving outside in the hallway. A moment later Veronica's brown loafers came into view.

It was too late. Veronica was waiting for him.

His cat, Tiger, crawled across his back and curled up comfortably on his neck. Then Tiger flicked his tail across Chris's nose. Chris was afraid he was going to sneeze.

The elevator door opened. "That's all right," he heard Veronica say. "I'll wait."

Twice more the elevator came to the floor and opened, and twice more Veronica let it go. The third time, however, he saw her brown loafers disappear into the elevator.

Peter was waiting for him at the corner. To Chris's relief, Veronica wasn't anywhere in sight.

"Hi, Chris!" Peter said.

Chris suddenly realized he hadn't saved any time to say, "Hello," or "How was your summer?" so he just said, "Ready for this one?"

Peter nodded. He knew immediately that Chris was talking about a joke. Together they began to walk to school.

"This guy is driving along the highway. . . ."

But Peter wasn't paying attention. He was looking back over his shoulder. Chris had a sinking feeling.

"Chris!" Veronica shouted. "I was so worried about you. I thought you were going to be late for school!"

Chris stared at her in amazement. She had appeared from nowhere. Then he realized she must have been sitting on the stoop across the street, watching the building.

Veronica squeezed her way between Chris and Peter. "I can't walk the whole way with you," she warned them. "I'll have to run back to catch the bus. Of course I'll miss the bus Hilary takes, but I don't mind."

"Go on," Peter said to Chris. He was trying to ignore Veronica, but it wasn't easy. She was taller than both of them, even though she was the same age — and she was walking right between them.

Chris and Peter dropped back a little. Veronica dropped back, too. The sidewalk was getting a bit crowded.

"So anyway. . . ." Chris tried very hard to concentrate. He tried to forget that Veronica was there. "This guy is driving along the highway with two penguins in the backseat of his car —"

Veronica gasped. "Is this true?" she asked.

"It's a joke," Peter said in disgust.

"Oh, I love jokes! Please tell *me!*" and she turned her full attention on Chris.

*       *       *

Veronica hated jokes. She never understood them. She thought they were babyish and a waste of time, but she wanted to show an interest. She knew that showing an interest and being a good listener was the fastest way to make friends. She had found a book in her grandfather's library in Vermont — a very old book called *How To Win Friends and Influence People*.

"So, anyway," Chris said, "this guy is driving along the highway with two penguins in the backseat of his car — "

"You already told us that part, Chris," Veronica whispered, trying to be helpful.

Chris looked annoyed, so Veronica kept quiet and worked on being a good listener.

"A policeman stops the guy and says, 'Hey! You've got two penguins in the backseat of your car!' The man says, 'I know. I don't know what to do with them.' So the policeman says, 'Why don't you take them to the zoo?' 'Good idea,' the man says, and drives off."

"Excuse me," Veronica said politely, "but don't you think he should call first?"

"Huh?" Chris asked.

"Shouldn't he call the zoo first and make an appointment — with the curator or someone like that? I don't think zoos take penguins right off the street."

"It's a joke, Veronica," Peter said.

"Even so . . . I think they need a medical checkup. . . ." Veronica stopped. Suddenly she felt terrible. She hadn't meant to interrupt. But, at the same time, she had become so *interested* in the situation Chris was describing. And being interested is the sign of a good listener, she told herself.

Chris took a deep breath and glanced at Veronica, who smiled at him in an encouraging way. He went on:

"The next day the policeman sees the man driving around again. The two penguins are still in the backseat. 'Hey!' the policeman says. 'I thought I told you to take them to the zoo!' 'I did,' the man says. 'I took them to the zoo yesterday. Today I'm taking them to the movies!' "

Veronica exploded with laughter. She shrieked. "I told you they couldn't get into the zoo without permission," and went off into gales of laughter.

Peter looked blankly at Veronica.

"Don't you get it?" Veronica asked Peter. "They

need *shots*. The zoo won't take new penguins without *shots*."

Peter looked puzzled. Veronica was delighted that she had understood the joke and Chris's best friend had not.

She turned to Chris and was impressed with the way Chris could keep a straight face. Chris looked very serious — too serious perhaps.

"That's a wonderful joke, Chris," Veronica said in her most sincere voice. Then she turned and ran happily to the bus stop.

# Kimberly

Veronica sat on the bus, feeling very pleased with herself. Of course she had only been practicing on Chris and Peter, but, to her surprise, she had actually enjoyed being a good listener.

She couldn't help thinking of ways to improve the joke:

— The penguins could be dressed in funny outfits. . . .

— The policeman could stop them for speeding. . . .

Veronica laughed out loud. A few people on the bus turned to look at her. She decided that, right after school, she would make a few modest suggestions to Chris. She was sure he would be interested in ways of making that joke a little funnier.

Veronica couldn't wait to get to school. Now that she knew the secret of making friends, she would be able to make friends with anyone she wanted to.

And this year, no matter what, Veronica was going to make friends with Kimberly Watson.

Kimberly was standing at the entrance to Maxton Academy. A group of boys and girls were clustered around her. Kimberly looked miserable. She kept twisting a piece of her long blonde hair around her finger and looking helplessly from one classmate to the other. Everyone seemed to be giving Kimberly advice:

"Why don't you. . . ."

"If I were you, I'd just tell them. . . ."

Her best friend, Amy, was trying to draw Kimberly away from the crowd. "Leave her alone," Amy was saying. "She doesn't want to talk about it."

Amy did not like sharing Kimberly with other people.

Veronica made her way toward the group. She wanted to give Kimberly advice, too, but she thought it might be a good idea to find out what was wrong first. "I'll be a good listener," she reminded herself.

"Hi, Veronica," said a little voice behind her. "I wanted to call you last night, but we got back too late."

Veronica turned around and saw Hilary standing on the school steps smiling at her.

Hilary was Veronica's best friend. Veronica had missed her terribly all summer. She had a million things to tell Hilary, but right now there was an emergency.

"What's wrong with Kimberly?" Veronica demanded.

Hilary shrugged. "I don't know." Hilary never took much interest in gossip. "How was California?" she asked Veronica.

"Fair," Veronica said, looking Hilary up and down. She couldn't help wishing that Hilary had done some improving over the summer. Hilary still wore her hair in a bunch on top of her head and carried her books in a flowered shopping bag.

"Only fair?" Hilary asked. "Didn't you have fun?"

"Oh, I had a wonderful time," Veronica said, "but I didn't exactly go to California. I went to

Vermont to visit my grandfather, instead."

Hilary looked puzzled. "I thought your father invited you to visit him in August."

"Well, he *wanted* to," Veronica explained, "but something came up."

"What?" Hilary asked.

Veronica hadn't the faintest idea. She hadn't heard from her father all summer.

"I'd rather go for Christmas vacation, anyway," Veronica said. "It's much nicer in Santa Barbara during Christmas. By the way, you're invited, too. You'll have to ask your parents right away so I can let him know."

"He invited me for Christmas, too?" Hilary asked.

"Well, he was trying to call all day yesterday, but Mrs. Moore knocked the phone off the hook when she was vacuuming."

"Then you *did* talk to him," Hilary said.

"Well, no," Veronica said, "but I know he was trying to call. The phone was off the hook for a whole three hours at least."

"Then how do you know he was trying to call?" Hilary asked.

"*Because the phone was off the hook!*" Veronica

was becoming impatient with Hilary. If Hilary couldn't even understand a simple thing like that. . . .

Hilary suddenly looked up and blinked. Her eyelids fluttered quickly. It was a habit that made Veronica uncomfortable. She wished Hilary would stop doing that. When they went to Santa Barbara, Veronica would insist that Hilary wear dark glasses all the time — even at night — so no one would notice.

Veronica looked over at Kimberly and found herself thinking how much better Kimberly would fit into life in Santa Barbara, California.

Veronica had never been to California, but she had a scrapbook full of pictures she had cut out of magazines. Kimberly looked just like a California girl with her long blonde hair, blue eyes, and suntan.

"I'll be right back," Veronica told Hilary, and she ran up the steps to join the group.

"What's the matter?" Veronica asked Meg, a chubby girl with orange-red hair, who was standing at the edge of the crowd.

Meg was indignant. "Kimberly's parents just

told her she was having a new baby brother or sister."

Veronica thought Kimberly Watson was the luckiest person in the world. Kimberly had everything: horseback riding lessons every day after school, a weekend house in the country, and a father who was always donating enormous amounts of money to Maxton Academy. And now she was getting a new baby brother or sister.

"Isn't she happy?" Veronica asked.

"Are you kidding?" Meg said. "They didn't even ask her if she wanted one."

"Oh," Veronica said.

"Kimberly hates babies," Meg went on. "She thinks babies are *disgusting*."

Veronica looked at Kimberly. It was clear that Kimberly needed her help.

Veronica squeezed her way to the front of the crowd right in front of Kimberly.

Amy spotted Veronica. "Look who's here," Amy said in a disgusted voice. "Veronica the Show-off."

Veronica did not pay any attention to Amy. She was sure that, if it weren't for Amy, she and Kimberly would have been friends long ago.

"I just heard the news," Veronica said quietly. She tried to look both stunned and sorrowful at the same time.

"Oh, mind your own business, Veronica," Amy said.

But Kimberly seemed to welcome the chance to tell someone new her troubles.

"Can you believe it?" Kimberly asked Veronica.

Veronica shook her head sadly.

"At my age!" Kimberly went on. "And, besides, they told me I could help choose a name for the baby, and they went right ahead and chose the names themselves — without even consulting me!"

"You're kidding!" Veronica said in a horrified voice. "What names did they pick?"

"Veronica," Amy muttered, "keep out of this."

Kimberly ignored Amy. "They picked Emily for a girl's name and Joseph for a boy's."

"How awful!" Veronica said.

"What's wrong with the name Joseph?" asked the boy who was standing next to Veronica.

Veronica turned on him. "How would *you* like to be named Joseph?" she asked the boy whose name she realized *was* Joseph.

There was no time to worry about details.

Veronica turned back to Kimberly. "I know *exactly* how you feel . . . *exactly* how you feel."

Kimberly was curious. "How?" she asked.

"You feel no one in the world cares the least little bit about *you*," Veronica explained.

"Well, they don't," Kimberly agreed. "The baby is due December eighteenth, and they tried to tell me it was my Christmas present." She groaned. "Just what I wanted."

It was working like magic. Kimberly was now addressing all her complaints to Veronica. Veronica was listening as hard as she could, nodding her head sympathetically, and murmuring things like, "How terrible!" and, "But they can't do that!" and, "I know just how you feel. . . ."

Suddenly Amy interrupted. "I know even more how she feels. I heard her parents talking. All they talk about is the baby this and the baby that."

Amy moved between Veronica and Kimberly so she was blocking Veronica's view. "Kimberly," Amy said, "I can just see it. Your mother and father and the new baby walking off into the sunset and *there you'll be!*"

"I know." Kimberly nodded her head hard. "I know!"

Kimberly seemed to enjoy that image so much Amy repeated it. Then she repeated it again for the benefit of the crowd: "*. . . and there she'll be!*"

Everyone began talking at once. Veronica tried to think of something equally depressing to cheer Kimberly up. One boy was suggesting a shocking picture of destruction: the baby tearing up the house, ruining all Kimberly's things, "and scribbling all over your homework."

But no one could match Amy's gloomy picture of life after the baby arrived: "walking off into the sunset and *there you'll be!*"

"Wait a minute!" Veronica suddenly said. "I just thought of something."

"Don't listen to her," Amy said.

"No, really," Veronica said. "I've just thought of the most awful thing, but," she said slowly, "I'm afraid it's true."

"No one's interested," Amy said, glancing at Kimberly.

"*I'm* interested," Kimberly said crossly.

Veronica was delighted. Was it possible that Kimberly was finally standing up to Amy?

"I don't know if I should say it; it's the most awful thing," Veronica said.

"*Please*, Veronica," Kimberly begged her.

"Well," Veronica began, "doesn't it seem a little bit . . . um . . . strange that your parents waited this long to have another baby?"

"I guess so," Kimberly said.

"They waited until you were a certain age, right?"

Kimberly looked puzzled. "Right," she agreed.

Veronica knew she was on to something. "They waited until you were just about old enough to baby-sit."

Kimberly was staring at Veronica.

"Don't you see?" Veronica had figured it out. "They won't have to pay a baby-sitter. They'll have *you!*"

Veronica now had the full attention of the crowd. "I hate to tell you this, Kimberly," she said, "but the only reason your parents had *you* was so that they would have a built-in baby-sitter for little Emily or Joseph!"

Everyone was furious. No one, not even Amy, could question the fact that Kimberly had been the victim of a clever plot.

"But that's slave labor!" Meg said.

"Of course," Veronica said smoothly, "and slavery is against the law."

Kimberly had turned pale. "Well, I won't do it. I won't baby-sit for that dumb kid."

"You'll have to," Veronica told her. "They'll make you." She sighed. "Well, I guess there's only one thing you can do."

"What?" Kimberly asked.

"Run away from home, of course," Veronica said.

Kimberly brushed her hair back and said coolly, "I was already thinking of doing that."

Veronica was surprised, but she suddenly had a wonderful idea. "I know! We can go live with my father in Santa Barbara."

"I didn't know your father lived in Santa Barbara." Kimberly was impressed. "I've been there. My aunt lives in Montecito. It's beautiful there."

"I know," Veronica said. She was already enjoying the picture of herself and Kimberly sunbathing on the beach, taking long walks by the ocean — becoming almost like sisters.

"Kimberly!" Amy said sharply. "You can't run away from home. Your parents will send the police after you."

"I don't even care," Kimberly said bitterly.

Veronica was getting nervous. If only there were some way of getting Kimberly to go with her just for Christmas vacation. Then she would be able to help Kimberly get over the shock of the new baby. She thought for a moment.

"Just a minute," she told Kimberly, and ran down the steps to where Hilary was waiting.

"Look, Hilary," Veronica said, "I'm not absolutely positive I'll be able to invite you to Santa Barbara for Christmas, so don't ask your parents yet, okay?"

Hilary looked puzzled. Veronica dashed back up the steps to where Kimberly and Amy stood.

They were arguing. "Don't be ridiculous," Amy was saying. "You can't run away from home."

"Amy's right," Veronica said suddenly.

Both girls turned to look at her.

"Look, Kimberly," Veronica said, "I don't think it *is* a good idea for you to run away from home — not right now."

Kimberly looked surprised.

"No," Veronica went on. "Wait until the baby is born. Then run away."

"I don't get it," Kimberly said dully.

"Don't you see?" Veronica explained. "They'll be so happy with the new baby, they won't even notice you're gone!"

Kimberly Watson had a funny expression on her face. A few seconds later she burst into tears.

Amy put her arm around Kimberly and led her toward the main entrance to the school. Kimberly was sobbing violently.

"Now look what you've done!" Amy called over her shoulder to Veronica.

# A Very
# Special Person

"But I can't apologize. I don't even know what I'm supposed to be sorry for," Veronica told Wingate Craven, the headmaster of Maxton Academy. "I was only trying to *help* Kimberly."

Veronica had never been in the headmaster's office before. She had been invited in "for a little chat" after Amy told the school secretary that not only had Veronica *made* Kimberly cry, she was trying to *make* Kimberly run away from home.

". . . but Kimberly was already thinking of doing that," Veronica explained, "and I didn't *make* Kimberly cry. I only said this tiny little thing and then, for no reason, Kimberly started to cry. You see," Veronica confided to the headmaster, "Kimberly is having problems at home."

Mr. Craven nodded. "Yes, Veronica, and I would be very interested in hearing how *you* feel we should handle this situation."

Veronica was pleased that the handsome young headmaster was asking for her advice. She was beginning to understand why all the parents were so impressed with him. "Wingate understands young people," they said. "He speaks their language."

"Well," Veronica began, "if I were you, I would have a talk with Kimberly's parents. They would listen to you. You see, Kimberly is feeling left out. They won't even let her choose the baby's name. She feels no one cares the least little bit about her. . . ."

"And is that how *you* feel, Veronica?" Mr. Craven asked softly.

Veronica thought about that. "Well, no. I think they care a little bit about Kimberly. They might be sorry if she got run over by a car, or something like that."

"Forget Kimberly for a moment," Mr. Craven said abruptly. "I'm more concerned about *you*."

"Me? But I'm not the one who's having problems at home!" Veronica laughed to show Mr. Craven just how ridiculous *that* idea was. "How could I?" she asked. "My mother's not even there. She's in Europe."

"I see," Mr. Craven said.

Veronica explained about the youth cure her mother was taking at the health resort. ". . . but she already looks so young, no one can believe she has *me*," Veronica said proudly.

"I see," Mr. Craven said again.

"What do you see?" Veronica asked suspiciously.

But Mr. Craven went on. "And what about your father? Your parents are divorced, aren't they?"

"*Happily divorced*," Veronica corrected him. "They're a *happily* divorced couple. My mother always gets the check right at the beginning of the month."

"And do you see your father often?"

"All the time," Veronica said cheerfully. "Well, almost all the time. During vacations mostly. Unless something comes up. My father happens to be a businessman."

"Oh," Mr. Craven said. "What sort of business is he in?"

"Oh, just a businessman," Veronica told him. "A regular one."

Veronica did not actually know what her father did. Her mother hardly ever talked about him. And, recently, Veronica had been having trouble remembering what he looked like. There were no pictures of him in the house.

"He looks just like Dwayne Cutler," Veronica told Mr. Craven.

"Who?" Mr. Craven asked.

"Dwayne Cutler — you know, on *In the Twilight of Darkness*."

"Is that a soap opera?" Mr. Craven asked.

"Yes," Veronica said. "It's Mrs. Moore's favorite. She's my baby-sitter. She's a lovely person and she does housework, too."

"Do you watch a lot of television?" Mr. Craven wanted to know.

"No," Veronica said, "but Mrs. Moore likes me to watch *Twilight of Darkness* with her. You see, we're both very worried about Felicity."

"Felicity?" Mr. Craven looked puzzled. "Oh, I see, she's a character on this *Twilight of Danger*."

*"Twilight of Darkness,"* Veronica corrected him. "Yes," she said sadly. "Felicity is ruining her life. You see, she's been going out with Brad, but Brad never got over being in love with Mavis. Meanwhile, Dwayne Cutler, the richest businessman in the town, is searching for his daughter and he doesn't even know that Felicity is his daughter even though they live in the same town — "

Mr. Craven cut her off. "Veronica," he said, "are you happy here at Maxton Academy?"

"Of course!" Veronica said. "I ought to be, for the money it costs." She tried to laugh the way her mother laughed, but it didn't seem to work. Mr. Craven was studying her thoughtfully.

He cleared his throat. "Um . . . as you know, Veronica, most of the boys and girls here at Maxton Academy came to us in nursery school. You joined us late — in the third grade, I believe."

Veronica's face felt hot. No matter what she did, she was sure she would always be "the new girl."

"We all feel, however, that you have shown a marked improvement in the last year. Your grades were good and everyone was very proud of the job you did in the spring musical."

The year before Veronica had played Eliza Doolittle in the school production of *My Fair Lady*. It was very unusual for a fourth-grader to be chosen for the starring role, but Veronica had an excellent singing voice and had no trouble remembering lines. The only problem was that she remembered other people's lines, too, and a few times she had said their lines as well as her own.

Veronica had been a great hit. The audience had clapped and cheered for her, but she had made a few enemies in the cast. Amy, for one, had only one line in the whole play, which, unfortunately, Veronica had remembered before Amy had a chance to say it.

"We were also quite proud of that letter you wrote to the newspaper about the closing of the Harding Branch of the public library," Mr. Craven went on. "That is exactly the sort of thing we encourage our students to do."

Veronica felt uncomfortable. She had gotten quite a lot of attention for writing that letter, which had been published in the daily newspaper. But the library still wasn't open, and her favorite librarian, Miss Markham, was out of a job.

(Of course Amy had been delighted that the library hadn't opened again. "You see, it didn't work! That proves it. Veronica only did it to show off!")

"Veronica," Mr. Craven said. "We at Maxton feel that you are a Very Special Person — a *Very Special Person*."

Veronica did not want to be a "Very Special Person"; she wanted to be friends with Kimberly Watson.

"Now, about Kimberly." Mr. Craven seemed to be reading her mind. "I'm going to level with you, okay?"

"Okay." Veronica felt a little better.

"I'm going to put it to you straight, okay?"

"Okay," Veronica said, and felt even more cheerful. Once again, Wingate Craven seemed to be treating her as an equal.

Mr. Craven leaned forward. "You're the one I'm thinking about, Veronica. And I feel that it's for *your* sake that an apology to Kimberly is needed. If you tell Kimberly you're sorry, it will make *you* feel better."

Veronica couldn't believe he was actually saying this. "But I can't tell her I'm sorry! If I tell her I'm sorry and I'm not, it will be *exactly* the same thing as telling a lie!"

Veronica was shocked at the idea of being *forced* to lie.

Wingate Craven seemed to be studying her with amusement. Veronica did not enjoy being studied with amusement.

"I won't do it," she said flatly. "I won't apologize to Kimberly."

Mr. Craven shrugged and began writing something on a legal pad. He murmured, "Of course you have to do what you think best. You know best, Veronica. The secretary will write you out a pass."

Veronica waited, but the headmaster did not look up again. He seemed to have forgotten all about her.

The entire school was in the auditorium for the opening assembly.

"I'll wait," Veronica whispered, but the sixth-grade teacher took her pass and told her to join her class.

Everyone turned to look as Veronica walked down the aisle. Suddenly she felt dizzy. She stopped and stared around at the blur of faces.

Then, out of the sea of faces she saw one face smiling at her. Hilary's face. Hilary was waving to her.

Veronica forced herself to walk on.

"I saved you a seat," Hilary whispered.

Veronica sat down next to Hilary.

"Are you all right?" Hilary whispered.

Veronica nodded, but she couldn't speak. Her chest felt tight and her eyes ached.

Someone was poking her in the back.

"If you're thinking about apologizing to Kimberly," Amy said in her ear, "forget it. Kimberly doesn't ever want you to speak to her again."

Veronica knew Amy and Kimberly were sitting right behind her, but she didn't even turn around.

Toward the end of the opening assembly, Miss Levy, the music teacher, announced that the musical this year would be *The Sound of Music*.

Everyone was very excited. It seemed to be everyone's favorite. Miss Levy waited for the auditorium to quiet down.

"Sign-up sheets for tryouts will be posted on the bulletin board in the lunchroom on Friday," Miss Levy told the students.

"I love *The Sound of Music*," Veronica heard Kimberly whisper to Amy. "I think I'm going to try out for Maria."

"Don't be ridiculous, Kimberly," Amy said. "You?"

"Well, why not?" Kimberly asked.

"I hate to tell you this, Kimberly," Veronica heard Amy say, "but you can't sing."

It was true. Kimberly had such a terrible voice, she was only allowed to mouth the words when the entire school sang Christmas carols each year. She sang through her nose in a loud monotone — every note was exactly the same.

But Veronica was sick and tired of listening to Amy. And she wanted to prove to Amy that she could talk to Kimberly Watson whenever she felt like it.

She turned around and looked right at Kimberly. "Anyone can learn to sing," she said.

Kimberly looked at Veronica in surprise.

"Veronica, I'm warning you . . ." Amy began.

But Veronica had turned around again.

"Well, it doesn't matter, anyway," Veronica heard Amy say. "Everyone knows Veronica's going to get the part of Maria. Just because she's better than everyone else. It isn't fair!"

"Maybe she won't try out," Kimberly whispered. "Maybe she'll give someone else a chance."

"Are you kidding?" Amy asked. "Veronica the Show-off?"

Veronica suddenly felt very tired. To her dismay she felt two big tears rolling down her cheeks. Veronica hardly ever cried. And she never cried in public.

To make matters worse, Hilary took her hand and held it tight. Why did Hilary have to be so nice to her? She held her breath and tried to keep back the tears.

". . . besides," Amy went on, "everyone knows Veronica is Miss Levy's favorite. . . ."

All of a sudden Hilary's voice rang out high and clear:

"Amy," she said, "shut up."

# In the Twilight
# of Darkness

Veronica stared at Hilary in amazement. It was not like Hilary to use language like that, but Hilary just gave Veronica a sweet smile.

Amy stopped talking, and she remained quiet for the rest of the day.

To her surprise, Veronica found herself somewhat of a heroine.

In gym class she was picked first for a soccer team. Veronica wasn't very good at soccer and she wondered how many people had seen her crying in assembly.

During recess a group of first-graders came up to her. The leader, a little girl named Kate, told Veronica that the first grade was on her side. As it turned out, they were not very clear about what had happened, but Amy had never been very nice to first-graders. "We all hate her," Kate told Veronica.

Word had spread that Amy had gotten Veronica into trouble. There were many people in the school who disliked Amy enough to offer Veronica a great deal of sympathy and understanding.

While she was waiting on line in the lunchroom, Veronica found herself surrounded by a group of boys.

"What did he *do* to you?" Jacob wanted to know. The boys at Maxton Academy had had far more experience with Wingate Craven and his "little chats" than the girls.

"Oh, I don't know," Veronica said shyly.

"Did he look at you like *this*?" Jacob pretended to be studying Veronica with amusement.

Veronica gasped. "Yes! How did you know?"

Jacob turned to the other boys. "He looked at her like *this*," and, once again, did an excellent imitation of Mr. Craven.

"Veronica! Veronica!" Sam said. "Did he say that you were" — Sam lowered his voice — " 'a Very Special Person'?"

Veronica nodded. She was somewhat surprised

that she wasn't the only "Very Special Person" at Maxton Academy.

Veronica was getting confused with all the kind attention she was receiving. She spent the rest of the day losing things or forgetting where she had put them. Hilary found her pencil case three times and ran back to the French classroom to get the gym suit Veronica had left there.

"Thank you," Veronica said. She felt very strange.

And the strangest thing of all — Veronica kept catching Kimberly looking at her thoughtfully all during social studies and language arts. She wondered if Kimberly was still thinking about running away to Santa Barbara.

At the end of the day Veronica was exhausted. When Hilary asked if Veronica would like to go over to her house, she shook her head. "Not today," she said.

Her head was spinning. People were being nice to her, but Veronica was afraid it was for the wrong reasons. She wondered how long it would last.

Veronica just wanted to be safe at home, watching *In the Twilight of Darkness* with Mrs. Moore.

\*　　　\*　　　\*

"That Brad!" Mrs. Moore shook her head sadly. "The way he treats Felicity!"

"It's disgusting!" Veronica said angrily.

Mrs. Moore and Veronica were sitting in the living room watching *In the Twilight of Darkness*.

Brad had been saying cruel things to Felicity all during dinner, and she got so upset, she went running out into the night.

It was only four o'clock in the afternoon, but the living room in Veronica's apartment was dark. Mrs. Moore kept the shades down and the curtains drawn all day so the furniture would not fade.

During the commercial, Veronica went into the kitchen to feed her cat, Gulliver. She was quite hungry herself, but she was only allowed to eat carrot sticks after school.

Veronica was big for her age, but she wasn't fat. Even so, her mother kept her on a permanent diet. Elaine Schmidt believed in what she called "a lifelong diet."

Veronica ate two carrot sticks and saved the rest for the next commercial break.

When she returned to the living room, Mrs. Moore was sniffing quietly.

"*I will not give up my search*," Dwayne Cutler was telling Mavis in his deep rich voice. "*I will find my daughter if it takes the rest of my life.*"

Mrs. Moore was sniffing quite loudly now. Veronica was disappointed. Every day she hoped this would be the day that Dwayne and Felicity would find out they were father and daughter.

When *Hospital Center* came on, Veronica left the room. She did not like *Hospital Center*.

She decided she would take her poodle out for a walk. She went to the front hall to get Lady Jane Grey's leash and saw a small package sitting on the front hall bench.

It was addressed to her.

The return address was a post office box in Santa Barbara, California.

Very carefully Veronica took off the brown paper without tearing the address. For months she had been asking her mother for her father's address, but her mother had told her that he was "in the process of moving."

There was a small box inside. Veronica opened it. She unwrapped the tissue paper and took out a small glass paperweight. Floating around in the paperweight was a tiny black top hat, a little carrot, and a few tiny pieces of coal.

In the box there was a note:

*Sorry I forgot your birthday. Hope this makes you laugh. Been terribly busy fixing up an old Victorian house. Lots of room. Hope to be settled by the end of November. Your loving Dad.*

Veronica looked at the paperweight and turned it upside down. She read a small label: CALIFORNIA SNOWMAN.

"But there's no snowman." Veronica couldn't figure it out. She put it carefully back into the box.

It didn't matter. She decided to write to her father and tell him it was the funniest present she had ever received. Then she would tell him that she would be absolutely delighted to visit him for Christmas and bring a friend.

For there was no doubt in Veronica's mind that this was an invitation for Christmas vacation. Why else would he tell her he would be settled by the end of November? And "lots of room" meant she should bring a friend!

Veronica was so excited she didn't know what to do first. She went into her room and unpacked the suitcase under the bed. She always kept it packed and ready to go to California. She began repacking, and checked to make sure her emergency pamphlets were there. One was called WHAT TO DO IF AN EARTHQUAKE STRIKES, and the other was HOW TO AVOID A RATTLESNAKE BITE.

Veronica was prepared for life in California.

Suddenly she realized she had better call Hilary right away and make sure she could go.

The line was busy. Veronica waited a few seconds and tried again just to make sure she had dialed the right number. Still busy.

A minute later she tried again — and then again.

Veronica called the operator to make sure Hilary's phone was not out of order. It wasn't.

Then she called the operator again and tried to convince her that it was an emergency and the operator had to break into Hilary's line immediately.

"Don't you see?" Veronica explained. "Hilary's

mother may be making other Christmas plans for her *right this minute!*"

The operator was very nice, but she told Veronica she was afraid that Christmas plans in September could not be considered an emergency.

Veronica had to tell *someone* besides the operator her exciting news.

She took the little package and went across the hall and knocked on Chris's door. There was no answer, so she rang the doorbell and banged a few times.

Chris opened the door. He took one look at Veronica and mumbled, "I have a lot of homework," and tried to close the door again.

But Veronica was already inside.

"I won't be here for Christmas," she announced, "and I have to know right away if you can feed Gulliver and Lady Jane Grey."

"But it's only September," Chris said, staring at Veronica.

"Well, can you or can't you?" Veronica tapped her foot impatiently.

"Do you have to know right this minute?" Chris asked.

Veronica nodded.

Chris's mother was in the darkroom behind the kitchen. Veronica followed Chris into the kitchen.

Chris's father made a living as a photographer and his mother often helped out with the printing of the photographs.

Chris knocked on the door. "Mom," he called, "can I feed Veronica's cat and dog over Christmas?"

There was a pause. "I guess so," Chris's mother called back.

Chris shrugged and turned to Veronica. "Okay," he said. He went back to the front door and held it open for Veronica.

"Wait a minute," Veronica said. "Don't you want to know where I'm going?"

Chris sighed. "Where are you going, Veronica?"

"To Santa Barbara — to visit my father!"

"That's nice," Chris said politely.

"But this time I really *am*." Veronica suddenly realized that she had told Chris this many times before, but she had never gone.

"Wait here," she told Chris. "I have to show you something."

"Does it have to be right now?" Chris asked.

"Yes," Veronica said, and she ran across the hall to get the package.

"First read this," she said, and handed Chris the note.

Chris read the note. Veronica watched him happily. "And you see," she explained, "he wants me to bring a friend."

"What makes you say that?" Chris asked.

" 'Lots of room' means bring a friend," Veronica said.

"Veronica," Chris said slowly, "it doesn't say 'lots of room'; it says, 'lots of *rooms.*' He means this house has lots of rooms."

"Don't be ridiculous." Veronica grabbed the note back and looked at it. There *did* seem to be an s on room. "He just made a little mistake," Veronica said. "He was trying to write too fast."

She felt annoyed at Chris. And she was sure her father's hand had slipped.

Chris shrugged. "I really have to do my homework."

"Wait," Veronica said, and she took the paperweight out of the box and showed it to Chris. She was delighted when Chris read the label and burst out laughing.

"That's terrific!" Chris said.

"I know," Veronica said proudly. "It's just too bad the snowman melted."

Chris stopped laughing and stared at Veronica. "But that's the joke, Veronica. Don't you get it? It's a California snowman. It's so hot there the snowman melted!"

"Of course I get it," Veronica said crossly, but she felt relieved that she now understood her birthday present. Then she remembered something.

"Oh, Chris, by the way, speaking of ice and snow. I was thinking about that penguin joke — "

"I don't want to talk about it," Chris said.

"But I have a few suggestions — "

Chris shut the door in her face. Veronica stood there for a moment. Then she called, "That's okay. I'll tell you another time."

She went back and tried Hilary again, but the line was still busy. She sat at her desk and wrote out a packing list for Hilary.

The phone rang. Veronica grabbed it.

"Hilary!" she shouted. "Listen, we have a

million things to do. First of all, we have to figure out what games we should take on the airplane. . . ."

There was a silence. Then a girl's voice said:

"This is Kimberly — Kimberly Watson."

# Veronica Bows Out

Veronica could not believe that Kimberly was actually calling *her*.

"Oh, hi, Kimberly." Veronica tried to sound as if Kimberly called her every night.

"I've been thinking about what you said," Kimberly said in a hesitant voice.

"You mean about running away to Santa Barbara?" Veronica was frightened.

"Oh, no!" Kimberly sounded embarrassed. "About what you said in assembly — you know, that anyone can learn to sing."

"Oh, that!" Veronica relaxed. "Well, you know, it's true and I ought to know. Don't listen to what Amy says."

"Oh, Veronica," Kimberly breathed. "Could you teach me to sing?"

46

"Of course," Veronica said smoothly. "You could learn in no time. I have taught quite a lot of my . . . um . . . friends to sing — from scratch!"

"Really?" Kimberly asked.

"Oh, yes," Veronica went on. "And many of my . . . um . . . students started with *terrible* voice problems — much worse than yours."

Veronica was thinking of the time she tried to teach her cat, Gulliver, to sing. After a week she was sure his howling had become much more musical.

"That's wonderful!" Kimberly said. She lowered her voice. "You see, I want to be Maria in *The Sound of Music* more than anything in the world."

"I see," Veronica said. "And you'd be *perfect* for the part — absolutely *perfect*." She paused. "But, of course I'll have to help you with the acting, too." What fun it would be to turn Kimberly into a star!

"Oh, Veronica!" Kimberly said. "I'm so happy you're not trying out for the part."

"I'm not?" Veronica had not quite understood that this was the price she would have to pay if she were to become Kimberly's acting and singing coach.

"Well, are you?" Kimberly asked.

"Oh, no," Veronica assured her. "I've had enough of all that. Of course it seemed glamorous when I was in the fourth grade, but now. . . ."

"Promise me you won't try out," Kimberly demanded.

"I promise," Veronica said.

"Good," Kimberly said. "Can we start right away? Can we have our first lesson on Saturday?"

"Saturday morning will be fine," Veronica told her. "I'll be at your house at ten."

"Wait a minute!" Kimberly said. "I don't want my parents to know about the lessons. It would be much better if we used the piano at *your* house."

"No problem," Veronica said cheerfully.

Veronica hung up the phone and sat there in a daze. She couldn't get over it. She had a date with Kimberly Watson!

After a while Veronica sat down at her desk and wrote a letter to her father, telling him how much she had laughed at the California snowman. "And it must have been pretty funny for you, too," she wrote, "when it melted right in front of your eyes."

Then she told him how excited she was about spending Christmas vacation in his new house in

Santa Barbara. She signed it: "Your loving daughter, Veronica Schmidt."

She thought for a moment and then she wrote a little P. S.: "I'm not exactly sure which friend I will invite to come with me, but I will let you know very soon."

Before she sealed the envelope, Veronica stuck in an extra copy of the pamphlet WHAT TO DO IF AN EARTHQUAKE STRIKES. She had been saving it to send to him as soon as she got his address.

She thought for a moment and wrote another P. S.: "I am enclosing this pamphlet just in case. You see, I had a terrible nightmare about you this summer."

In the dream her father — looking exactly like Dwayne Cutler in *Twilight of Darkness* — was trapped in an earthquake. Veronica was running to save him, but the sidewalk kept opening up in big cracks in front of her. The dream was over before Veronica could rescue her father from the collapsed building.

Veronica had a quiet dinner with Mrs. Moore in front of the TV watching a game show, and then she went to bed. But she had trouble going to sleep. There were a few problems she would have to work out before Kimberly's first singing lesson on Saturday.

For one thing, Veronica did not know how to play the piano and that bothered her a bit. But she was sure that, with a little practice, she would be able to pick out tunes. Besides, Kimberly probably wouldn't even notice if she faked it a little. Miss Levy, the music teacher, had once said that she was afraid that Kimberly was completely tone deaf.

"Lucky for me," Veronica told herself sleepily.

She found herself thinking how delighted her mother would be to hear that Veronica had a date with Kimberly Watson. Veronica's mother had once worked with Kimberly's father to raise money for the symphony, and she often asked about "the Watson girl" and why didn't Veronica see more of her.

Her mother had also asked Veronica a few times if her friend Hilary wasn't "a bit odd."

But there was another problem, a more serious one. Even though her mother had often talked about Veronica taking piano lessons, there was no piano in their apartment. Veronica was certain her mother would approve of getting a piano, but she wasn't returning home from Europe until Friday morning.

The piano simply had to be there Saturday morning when Kimberly arrived. Veronica knew she would have to make the arrangements for the piano by herself, before her mother got back.

Veronica woke up the next morning with a plan.

"Miss Levy," Veronica said after school that afternoon, "my mother asked me if you know where we could rent a piano. You see, we need it right away because — guess what!"

"What?" Miss Levy had seemed pleased when she found Veronica waiting for her in the music room after school.

Veronica took a deep breath. "I'm starting piano lessons on Saturday."

The music teacher was very happy for Veronica. "That's simply marvelous, Veronica," she said. Then she told Veronica she would call her "little man" who repairs pianos and find out from him where Veronica's mother could rent a piano in a hurry.

"Now, does your mother want to rent an upright like that — " Miss Levy pointed to the dark wood piano against the wall in the music room " — or a baby grand?"

Veronica was delighted to hear there was such a thing as a baby piano — a miniature piano. There wasn't much room in her living room, so she said, "A baby grand, please."

"Are you sure?" Miss Levy asked. "It costs a lot more per month."

That made sense to Veronica. People living in city apartments would be willing to pay more for tiny pianos. And they were probably quite delicate. Veronica would be very careful.

"She definitely said she wanted a baby grand," Veronica told Miss Levy.

Miss Levy took Veronica's home telephone number and told her she would call her later that afternoon.

As Veronica was leaving the music room, Miss Levy said, "By the way, Veronica, I think you will make a wonderful Maria in *The Sound of Music*."

"Shouldn't someone else get the chance?" Veronica asked nervously.

"Well, that's very generous of you, Veronica," Miss Levy said somewhat sharply, "but our standards are high and we will choose the best person for the part. Here at Maxton our productions are always *professional*." She looked at Veronica, "You *are* planning to try out, aren't you?"

Veronica didn't know what to say. Kimberly had made her promise she wouldn't try out.

Then she got an idea. "Oh yes, I'll sign up for the tryouts," she promised. She figured she could sign up and then find some excuse for backing out later — a broken arm or something like that.

"Good," Miss Levy said. "The sign-up sheets will be posted on Friday, but the tryouts aren't until right before Thanksgiving. You will have plenty of time to prepare — especially with your new piano." She smiled at Veronica.

"That's what I was thinking," Veronica said.

Hilary was waiting for her on the front steps.

"Not today," Veronica said once again when Hilary invited her to her house. She knew she had to be home when Miss Levy called.

"But Melody's coming," Hilary said, as they started walking together. "She wants to see you. She called last night and said she thought we should start a children's committee right away to try to get the Harding Branch of the library opened again."

"Really?" Veronica was excited. Melody was a friend they had met at the library the year before. She had helped on the letter Veronica wrote to the newspaper, protesting the closing of the library.

"Well, just tell Melody we'll have to do it tomorrow," Veronica told Hilary. "I can't do it today."

Hilary shook her head. "Melody's coming to my house right from school."

"Well, you're not planning to talk about the library without *me!*" Veronica was horrified.

Hilary didn't say anything. All at once Veronica found herself telling Hilary about Kimberly and how she was going to train Kimberly for the lead in *The Sound of Music*. "You see, I'm only doing it to help Kimberly get over her problems at home," Veronica explained, feeling very noble. "How would *you* feel if your parents decided to have a baby without even consulting you?"

Hilary listened quietly. When Veronica finished, she said, "I don't think you can do it. I don't think anyone can teach Kimberly to sing. Besides,

Kimberly can never remember lines. You know how she is in French class."

"Of course I can do it," Veronica said.

Hilary was grave. "Veronica, you've got to stop Kimberly from trying out. She'll make a fool of herself."

"Don't be ridiculous!" Veronica laughed loudly. "Anyone can try out. You know, Hilary, it *is* a free country."

They walked another block in silence.

"Anyone can learn to sing," Veronica said.

A block later she said, "And you have to give people a chance. At least I have some *faith* in Kimberly."

Hilary didn't say anything.

Veronica found herself staring at the flowered shopping bag Hilary used as a book bag.

"You know, Hilary," Veronica said, "if I were you, I'd ask for a real book bag for your birthday. You can't carry your books in a shopping bag for the rest of your life."

"I don't like book bags," Hilary said.

"Of course you do," Veronica assured her. "Everyone at Maxton has a book bag. If I were you — "

"But you're not," Hilary said quietly. "You're not me."

Veronica was so angry at Hilary that by the time they reached Hilary's corner, she said in her coldest voice, "And I think it's terribly unfair of you and Melody to go saving the library *behind my back*."

Hilary sighed. "Oh, come on, Veronica," but Veronica kept walking very fast.

A minute later she looked quickly over her shoulder to see if Hilary was running after her — trying to stop her — but the street was deserted.

# The Making of a Star

"I don't get it," Kimberly whispered angrily. "You *promised* me you weren't going to try out."

"I'm not going to," Veronica said coolly.

*"But you just signed up for Maria!"*

It was Friday noontime. Veronica and Kimberly were standing in the hallway outside the lunchroom.

Hilary stopped by to ask Veronica if she would like her to save her a seat in the lunchroom.

"That's okay," Veronica said politely. "Thank you so much for asking me."

"You're welcome," Hilary said just as politely and went inside.

Ever since Tuesday, Veronica and Hilary had been very formal with one another. Hilary had called her once to tell her about the meeting with

Melody about the library, but Veronica had told her she had to get off the phone right away — in case Kimberly was trying to reach her. Hilary had not called again.

Kimberly was furious with Veronica. "Erase your name," she demanded. "Erase it right this minute. You *promised*."

Veronica looked Kimberly up and down with approval. Kimberly looked terrific. Her blonde hair was in long braids that were wrapped around her head. Veronica had tried to convince her to cut it off. "Maria starts out as a nun in a convent," Veronica had argued, "and nuns cut their hair all off." She had finally gotten Kimberly to agree to the braids.

Veronica and Kimberly had been on the phone for hours the night before, discussing what Kimberly would wear on Friday to sign up for the tryouts for *The Sound of Music*.

"But the tryouts aren't until November," Kimberly kept saying.

"It's all part of becoming a star," Veronica had explained. "Getting into the role . . . really *feeling* like Maria. You want people to look at you and *think* Maria!"

Kimberly was wearing Veronica's dirndl, an Austrian peasant dress that Veronica's mother had brought back from Europe a long time ago. It was a little short, but Veronica thought Kimberly looked adorable.

". . . and those braids really work," Veronica said.

"Well, I feel ridiculous," Kimberly said. She glared at Veronica. "And don't change the subject!"

". . . but you really should act a little more perky," Veronica went on. "Maria is a very perky person. And she absolutely loves children. That's how she got to be governess for Baron von Trapp's children."

Veronica had given this a lot of thought. She had spent every afternoon playing her record of *The Sound of Music.*

"In fact," Veronica continued, "I was thinking of setting up something with the kindergarten, during recess or something like that. Picture this: There you are leading them around the playground, singing, 'Doe-a-Deer-a-Female-Deer,' and patting them on their heads."

"Veronica!" Kimberly said in a warning voice.

"Look, Kimberly," Veronica said, "I am not going to try out, but I had to sign up."

Kimberly looked at Veronica with distrust.

"Don't you see? Miss Levy would get suspicious if I didn't sign up."

"So?" Kimberly asked.

"But the *real* reason I had to sign up," Veronica went on, "is that my name will scare other people away. No one else will dare sign up to try out for Maria."

Veronica was sure this was true. Many of her classmates had already told her that they *knew* she was going to get the part.

Kimberly thought it over. "Maybe you're right," she said. She thought some more. "But then what?"

"Well," Veronica said slowly, "right before tryouts, I'll find some excuse to get out of it — a broken arm or something like that," she said casually.

"A broken leg would be better," Kimberly suggested.

Veronica smiled at Kimberly. Kimberly was finally catching on.

Now everything was under control. Her mother was on her way home from the airport right this minute. She would have a few hours to rest and get over her jet lag before Veronica came home. (Veronica had even called the airport to make sure her mother's flight was due in on time.)

The piano would not be delivered until five-thirty in the evening. That gave Veronica more than two hours to explain the piano to her mother, even though she felt she didn't really need that much time. Her mother would be refreshed when it came time for them to rearrange the furniture in the living room to make way for the piano.

Kimberly was looking at Veronica with a mixture of admiration and curiosity.

"How are you planning to break your arm?" she asked Veronica.

Veronica stared at Kimberly. Did Kimberly expect her to actually break her arm just so she could play Maria in *The Sound of Music*?

"You know," Kimberly went on in a dreamy voice, "my cousin Nicholas fell off the top of the slide in the playground and broke his arm so badly he was in a cast for months. The top part of his arm. It's much better to break the top part of your arm — more painful, too," she explained to Veronica. "And the cast itched him so much he almost went crazy. But then, of course, my cousin

Rebecca got *her* arm slammed in a car door — "

"That's nice." Veronica cut her off. Kimberly's enthusiasm was bothering her. She was anxious to change the subject.

"Don't worry, Kimberly. I'll think up some excuse. Now." Veronica became businesslike. "It's your turn to sign up."

Kimberly gasped. "But I can't! Everyone will laugh at me!"

"No one will laugh at you," Veronica said gently. She took Kimberly by the shoulders. "Look at me!" she said.

Kimberly looked at Veronica and blinked her beautiful long lashes.

Veronica was very pleased with the way she was handling Kimberly. After all, her most important job was to give Kimberly courage and support. She had to show Kimberly she had faith in her.

"They'll make fun of me," Kimberly murmured.

Veronica spoke slowly. "Listen to me, Kimberly. *No one will make fun of you. No one will laugh at you.* Do you understand?"

Kimberly nodded and went inside the cafeteria.

Suddenly Veronica heard Amy shriek. "What are you doing, Kimberly? Are you crazy?"

"Let go of my arm!" Kimberly shrieked back.

The entire lunchroom exploded with laughter. Veronica froze. More laughter.

It was at this point that Veronica decided that this might be a good day to skip lunch. How delighted her mother would be if Veronica had lost a pound or two while she was away.

As she was tiptoeing in the direction of the girls' bathroom, Kimberly came flying out of the cafeteria. Her face was bright red, and she was out of breath.

"I signed my name!" Kimberly gasped. "I signed my name, but it came out a squiggle because Amy tried to stop me!"

Veronica could hardly speak. "Kimberly," she whispered, "I'm proud of you — very, very proud!"

# The Telegram

The minute Veronica walked in the door of her apartment she knew something was wrong.

Mrs. Moore was sitting in her favorite chair watching *The Young and the Breathless*, the soap opera that came on before *Twilight of Darkness*.

It was three-thirty in the afternoon. If Veronica's mother were here, Mrs. Moore would have left by now. Besides, Mrs. Moore would never let Veronica's mother catch her in front of the TV.

Veronica stared at the telegram on the front hall table. She opened it.

DARLING:

HAD TO CATCH A LATER FLIGHT. HOME FOR DINNER. ELAINE.

For the past year Veronica's mother had been asking Veronica to try to call her by her first name. It made her feel younger. But Veronica sometimes forgot.

"Mommy," she whispered, "how can you do this to me?"

Veronica went into the living room and sat down to think about the piano that was arriving in less than two hours.

The man who had called from Baldwin Piano had told her it would be perfectly fine if she wrote a check to cover the first month's rental and delivery charges. (He had assumed that Veronica was her mother on the phone, and Veronica had found it simpler to let him believe that.) After all, he had said, they were friends of Miss Levy, the music teacher.

The piano simply had to be delivered this evening; it had to be there when Kimberly arrived for her first singing lesson tomorrow morning.

But what about the check?

"My mother will drop the check off first thing Monday morning," Veronica heard herself telling the deliverymen.

The man had also said that his deliverymen

could not be expected to move any furniture around in the apartment.

Veronica sat in the middle of the big white couch and looked around the living room. She wondered just how big this baby piano was. There was very little wall space. Large windows covered two whole walls, and the rest of the wall space was taken up by bookcases, tables, china cabinets, and the long white couch she was sitting on.

She had very little choice. She would have to move the couch toward the bookcase. That would make about four feet between the couch and the window. A little piano would look quite nice there, she thought, with the light filtering in through the big window and the hanging plants.

Veronica stood up and began pushing the couch. The couch wouldn't budge. She tried again with all her might.

"I think I lost something behind the couch," she called to Mrs. Moore, but Mrs. Moore was too deeply involved in what was happening on *The Young and the Breathless*. Veronica thought that if two elephants walked in right now and sat on the couch, Mrs. Moore probably wouldn't notice.

Veronica sat on the floor between the window

and the couch and tried to move the couch by pushing at it with both legs. No luck.

She stood up. She needed help and she knew it. Veronica went to the telepone and dialed Hilary's number. But Hilary wasn't home.

"She went to her lesson," Hilary's mother told Veronica.

"Oh, no," Veronica said. "I forgot."

Hilary took karate lessons and was quite strong, even though she looked delicate. Veronica was sure that she and Hilary together could move that couch.

"What time will her lesson be over?" Veronica asked in a faint voice.

"Not until four-thirty," Hilary's mother told her.

"Oh, no!" Veronica wailed. "What am I going to do?"

"Is everything all right, Veronica?" Hilary's mother sounded worried. "Is there anything *I* can do?"

"No, thank you. Everything's just fine." But Veronica's voice was trembling.

"Look, Veronica," Hilary's mother said, "if, by any chance, she calls me before she leaves her lesson, I'll have her call you right away. Otherwise, she'll call you as soon as she gets home."

"Yes, please," Veronica whispered. "Please have her call me."

"I certainly will," Hilary's mother said.

Veronica hung up. She went and sat on the couch again. *In the Twilight of Darkness* had already started and Dwayne Cutler, looking very handsome in his three-piece suit, was paying a visit to the adoption agency.

*"But the records have to be here,"* Dwayne was saying in his deep rich voice. *"The papers can't be missing!"*

The woman at the adoption agency told Dwayne that even if they were there, he would not be allowed to see them.

Veronica was horrified. How would Dwayne ever find out that Felicity was his daughter? She sat there, her eyes fixed on the TV.

During the first commercial break, Veronica went and got her carrot sticks.

During the next break, she went into the front hall to see if a letter had come from her father. There was no letter. Veronica was pretty sure he'd call sometime over the weekend.

She watched the rest of the program and suddenly realized, when *Twilight of Darkness* was over, that she'd let a whole half hour slip by. What had she been thinking of? Hilary would get home much too late to help.

Veronica went across the hall and knocked on Chris's door. She waited. Then she rang the doorbell and kept her finger on it for a while. With the other hand she banged on the door.

"Quick!" she called. "It's me, Veronica. I have an emergency!"

Chris opened the door. He looked embarrassed to see Veronica. "What do you want?" he asked.

"Is someone here?" Veronica asked.

"Peter's here," Chris told her. "We're very busy doing homework."

"Well, that's too bad," Veronica said. "This time it's really an emergency."

Chris sighed. "Now what, Veronica?"

Veronica started talking very fast. "You see, this piano is coming and my mother doesn't even know because she took a later flight and she won't be here until dinner and this piano is coming for dinner. . . ." Veronica was getting all mixed up.

Chris grinned. "A piano is coming for dinner?"

"Yes," Veronica said. "I mean, *no!* You see, a

piano is coming and the couch won't move and. . . ."

Chris was still grinning. "Sure, Veronica," he said. "A piano is coming to your house. Do you expect me to believe that?"

"Of course," said another voice. Peter had suddenly appeared behind Chris. "Don't you see, Chris," Peter said. "A piano is coming to Veronica's house for dinner and the couch absolutely refuses to move." Peter turned to Veronica. "Is the couch having dinner, too? Oh, I see, you don't have anything to feed the piano. Now that *is* a problem."

Veronica was so angry she couldn't speak. She glared at the two boys. Chris was now laughing so hard, he had to lean against the door to keep from falling down.

He managed to gasp, "Well — I'll — look — in the refrigerator, but I don't think we have much in the way of piano food — "

"I'm serious!" Veronica yelled. "A piano is coming here. You've got to believe me!"

"Order out," Peter suggested. "A pizza, or maybe some Chinese food." He turned to Chris, who was now howling with laughter.

"Do pianos like pizza?" he asked.

Just then Veronica heard the elevator door open behind her. She turned around.

"Hilary!" she shouted. "You got here just in time!"

# P-I-A-N-O

Hilary's cheeks were pink. She was out of breath. "I came straight from karate," she told Veronica. "Mama called me there. She's worried that something's wrong."

Veronica managed to give Chris and Peter a withering look before she said, "Hilary, I think we'd better go inside and discuss this."

It was quarter to five. Mrs. Moore was watching *Hospital Center*. Veronica tried to keep her voice down. "Remember the piano I told you about?"

Hilary's face was blank. "The piano?" she asked.

"Yes!" Veronica said, "the *piano* — the P-I-A-N-O!"

Hilary shook her head. Veronica suddenly realized that, although she had told Hilary about Kimberly's singing lessons, she had never mentioned the piano.

Time was running out. "Hilary," Veronica said, "do you think you could help me move that couch over there? It's very heavy."

Hilary shrugged. "Sure," she said.

Veronica could have hugged Hilary for not asking any more questions.

Mrs. Moore wanted to start dinner, so Hilary and Veronica helped her get the TV into the kitchen.

Hilary studied the problem. She tested the couch to see how heavy it was.

"Pie plates," she said. "Do you have any metal pie plates? We'll need four of them."

Veronica nodded and ran to fetch them.

Hilary took charge. While Hilary lifted each leg, Veronica slipped a pie plate under it. Suddenly the couch was quite easy to move. It slid right along the white carpet and right up against the side of the bookcase.

Veronica sighed. "Hilary, you saved my life. You see, this piano is being delivered in — " she looked at her watch " — thirty minutes."

"A piano?" Hilary asked. "But a piano won't fit there!" She pointed to the space between the window and the couch.

"It's just a tiny piano," Veronica explained, "a

miniature. I guess it's the latest thing in . . . um
. . . technology. It's called a baby something or
other."

"A baby grand?" Hilary asked.

"That's it!" Veronica said.

"Veronica, a baby grand is enormous. It won't
fit there. It won't fit in this room at all."

"Of course it will," Veronica said, but she had
the feeling Hilary knew what she was talking
about.

"*We* have a baby grand," Hilary explained.

Veronica gasped. The piano in the family room
at Hilary's house stood in the center on three legs
and took up most of the floor space. Veronica muttered, "Well, you would have thought they could
have called it a grown-up grand or something like
that."

She looked at Hilary in desperation. "What do
we do now?" she asked.

Hilary sized up the situation in a hurry. "The
only way that piano will fit is if the couch goes
out of the living room."

"The couch goes," Veronica said at once.

The couch was quite easy to move with the pie
plates under the legs. Veronica and Hilary slid it

across the carpet and into the hallway in no time.

"Turn left," Veronica told Hilary.

It was a tight fit, but they managed to slide the couch all the way down the hallway.

"Where are we putting it?" Hilary asked.

Veronica stopped. She hadn't gotten up to thinking about that yet. At the end of the hallway was a bathroom.

"We're leaving it here," Veronica said.

"In the middle of the hallway?" Hilary asked. "But how will you and your mother get to the bathroom?"

"Easy," Veronica said. "Watch me. All you have to do is take off your shoes, like this — " Veronica took off her shoes " — walk across the couch, like this — " Veronica showed her " — and put your shoes back on again and go to the bathroom. Simple!"

Hilary looked doubtful.

It was quarter past five. "We'll worry about the couch later," Veronica told her.

But Hilary had to leave. She had told her mother she would be home by now.

Veronica lay on the couch and waited for the piano. She had become very excited about getting a real piano — the kind they use in big concert halls. Kimberly would be very impressed. And she was sure her mother would be delighted.

Veronica imagined herself sitting at the piano, just the way Hilary's older sister, Samantha, sat there, very straight, her hair pulled back with a bow, perhaps, her hands poised above the keyboard. . . .

At five-thirty the intercom rang. The deliverymen were on their way up.

Veronica ran to the window. Her heart leaped when she saw the piano being rolled down the ramp of the big truck. The piano was on its side on a dolly. It looked enormous.

A few seconds later her doorbell rang.

A big man named Rudy seemed to be in charge of the other two men.

"We're going to bring it up in the service elevator," he told Veronica. He stopped and looked at their front hall.

"Hey," he said, "why didn't they tell us the hallway was at right angles to the door? We're going to have to take off the front door."

"Okay," Veronica said. A man whose name was Gino began taking off the front door.

The noise of the front door of Veronica's apartment being taken off attracted Chris and Peter. They stood in the hallway in complete silence, watching the operation.

"Where's the piano going?" Rudy asked Veronica.

Veronica showed him the nice big empty space in the living room, and he seemed to approve.

"Good windows, too," Rudy said thoughtfully.

"Thank you," Veronica said, and wondered why he was talking about windows.

Just then the elevator door opened and one of the men Veronica had seen lifting the piano off the truck stepped out.

"Look," he said to Rudy, "that service elevator won't take it. Not wide enough."

Rudy made a quick decision. "We still have some daylight," he said. "We'll use the hoist. Gino can get the hoist up on the parapet. It should be a pretty smooth operation."

He turned to Veronica. "Where's your mother?" he asked.

"In the kitchen," Veronica mumbled.

Rudy called through the kitchen door. "We're going to have to put a hoist up on the roof, Mrs.

Schmidt. I hope it's all right if we remove the living room window."

Mrs. Moore didn't answer. She was clattering around in the kitchen, which Rudy took as a sign that it would be okay.

Veronica stood in the front hallway and watched as the men took down the hanging plants and removed the large living room window along with the window frame.

"I don't get it," she said.

Chris was very excited. "Veronica! They're going to hoist it up from the roof on pulleys, and bring it in through the living room window!"

Chris and Peter went over to the open window and watched the operation from there.

Veronica held very still. She was afraid Chris and Peter would get so excited they would fall out the window.

"Look at that!" Peter said. "They have a man on the roof across the street. They're going to use a guideline so the piano won't bang against the building."

Chris said, "Now they're putting big ropes around the piano. Don't you want to see this, Veronica?" He made room for her at the window.

Veronica shook her head.

"We've got to go down to the street to watch this part," Peter said.

"We'll be right back," Chris told Veronica.

Veronica went to the window and peeked down at the street.

Just at that moment she saw a taxi pull up behind the big van.

Her mother stepped out of the taxi and waited for the driver to help her with her bags.

Veronica thought her mother looked wonderful. She looks so young! she thought. Her mother was wearing a royal blue knit dress. Her dark shiny hair had been cut in a short bob.

When her mother stepped out of the elevator, Veronica ran to greet her.

"Darling, I'm home," Elaine Schmidt said.

Chris and Peter stepped out of the elevator, too, along with one of the deliverymen and three piano legs.

Elaine Schmidt looked around her. "I don't know what's going on," and she laughed her beautiful laugh.

Veronica remembered to call her mother by her first name.

"Elaine," she said, "you look wonderful. Your face looks so . . . um . . . fresh . . . so fresh and *radiant!*"

It really did. Her mother's complexion was just like peaches and cream. "I hardly recognized you," Veronica went on. Chris and Peter, she noticed, were still watching the whole scene.

"Where's our front door?" Veronica's mother asked.

She walked into the front hallway and looked down the hall. "What's the living room couch doing there?" she wanted to know.

"Oh, I'll explain," Veronica said, but her mother had already walked through the archway to the living room. Veronica began telling her about Kimberly and the singing lesson.

"What does Kimberly Watson have to do with the window in our living room?" Her mother spoke in a very controlled voice. "It's missing."

Veronica's mother had still another question:

"Veronica, what is that man doing in our living room?"

Veronica moved around to block her mother's view and tried once again to explain.

But her mother wasn't listening. She was staring past Veronica, her eyes opened wide.

Veronica had her back to the window. But she knew that when her mother's face turned from peaches and cream to an ashen gray, it was, most likely, at this very minute that a piano was coming through their living room window.

"You should have seen it, Mom!"

Chris and his mother were having breakfast early Saturday morning.

"It came in the window and went right out again! Veronica's mother just told those men that the piano 'was going right back where it came from!' "

Chris hadn't been able to stop talking about Veronica's piano, as he called it.

"Poor Veronica," his mother said.

"Her mother didn't even scream," Chris went on. "She just went and wrote an enormous check for the delivery and first month's rent. Then she said something real quiet to Veronica and went to lie down!"

"Elaine's a cool cookie," his mother said, and began clearing away the breakfast dishes.

She stopped and turned to Chris. "Well, I don't know if Veronica will be allowed out today, but wouldn't it be nice if we invited her to do something with us — go to a movie or something?"

"Are you crazy?" Chris asked. "Go to the movies with Veronica? What if someone sees me?"

His mother shrugged.

Chris got dressed. Then he went to the front door and waited for Veronica to take her poodle for her morning walk.

He got on the floor and put his eye right up against the crack under the door and waited.

Ten minutes later he saw Veronica's brown loafers and Lady Jane Grey's little white paws.

"Oh, hi, Veronica," Chris said as he slipped out into the hallway.

Veronica seemed to be thinking about something else.

"Listen, Veronica," Chris went on, "I'm really sorry I didn't believe you."

"Huh?" Veronica asked.

"I'm really sorry I didn't believe a piano was coming to your house."

Veronica seemed to be in a trance.

\*        \*        \*

Chris managed to be dumping the kitchen garbage pail in the hallway trash can when Veronica and Lady Jane Grey returned from their walk.

"Are you getting punished?" Chris asked as casually as he could. He simply *had* to know.

Veronica nodded.

"What's the punishment?" Chris asked.

Veronica looked him straight in the eye.

"No Halloween," she said.

"You mean no costume — no trick-or-treating?" Chris was aghast.

Veronica nodded again.

Chris couldn't believe any mother in the whole world could have dreamed up such a punishment.

He watched Veronica open the door to her apartment.

"Just a minute!" he called.

Veronica turned around.

"Um . . . you see, we *were* thinking about going to the movies today, but all that's playing is *The Sound of Music*," Chris said, "so I guess you don't want to see that. You've probably seen it a million times."

*"The Sound of Music?"* Suddenly Veronica's face lit up. "Well, then, I'll take Kimberly to *The Sound*

*of Music*! That's what I'll do with her. We'll sit through it a few times. And — I know!"

Chris was worried about Veronica. She seemed to be talking to herself.

". . . this morning we'll go to the hill in the park and practice singing in the open air," Veronica went on, "just like Maria!" Veronica spread her arms wide and sang, "The hills are alive — with the sound of music. . . ."

Chris stared at Veronica. He wondered if the punishment had been too much for her, but suddenly she stopped singing.

"Thank you very much, Chris," Veronica said in her most sincere voice, "but I'm afraid I have other plans for today."

Chris watched her go into her apartment and thought that, in some way, Veronica was a very brave person. He was sure that every kid, no matter *what* he did, had the *right* to Halloween.

Chris made up his mind that he would be especially nice to Veronica on Halloween.

# The Hills
# Are Alive. . . .

Veronica and Kimberly sat through two showings of *The Sound of Music* that Saturday afternoon. They both cried when it was over.

The following Saturday they went again, sat through two more showings, and cried some more.

In the mornings they went to the park to practice singing on a hill overlooking the duck pond. These lessons "in the open air," as Veronica liked to say, went on long after *The Sound of Music* had stopped playing at the local movie-theater.

It was a bright Saturday morning the week before Halloween. Kimberly seemed a bit chilly in the Austrian peasant costume, but she refused to wear the woolen shawl Veronica had brought to the park for her.

Veronica was wearing her "rehearsal clothes" —
a black turtleneck sweater and jeans.

"You see, all you have to do for the tryouts is
learn one scene perfectly," Veronica explained,
"and just one song. Once you get the part, I'll
teach you the rest. In fact, we can practice on the
beach in Santa Barbara over Christmas vacation."

"Ooops," Kimberly said with a giggle. "I forgot
to ask my parents again. I'll ask them tonight if I
can go. I promise I won't forget."

"That's okay," Veronica said. She hadn't heard
from her father yet, anyway. But she knew how
busy he must be, getting the new house ready for
her visit. She was sure that, as soon as he was
settled in November, he would send the plane
tickets.

"Do I have to do the opening number?" Kimberly asked. "I'd much rather do the scene with
'Doe-a-Deer-a-Female-Deer' in it."

Veronica sighed and looked at Kimberly. It had
taken Kimberly over a month just to learn the
words to the opening number. Kimberly forgot
lines easily, and Veronica had to test her every
night over the phone.

"We'll go over it again," Veronica said firmly.

She began reading from the back of the record cover:

"Evening is approaching. The busy nuns are going about their daily tasks. But Maria is not among them. Maria is out in the mountains enjoying nature and the sound of music in the air. . . ."

Kimberly broke in: "My parents are shopping for wallpaper for the baby's room today. They said I could help choose it, but I told them I wasn't the least bit interested."

Veronica listened sympathetically to Kimberly's complaints. She thought it was important for Kimberly to talk over the problems she was having at home before they began to work.

"How do I know what kind of wallpaper this dumb baby is going to like, anyway?" Kimberly asked. "It's not even born yet!"

"Good point," Veronica said. "So, anyway, you start by running onto the mountain, enjoying nature. You sniff a couple of flowers. Hug the tree over there. Then you stop and look up at the sky, take a deep breath of fresh mountain air, and throw off your nun's habit. Then you open your arms wide, like this — " Veronica showed her " — and burst out singing:

"The hills are ali-i-ive
With the sound of mu-u-u-sic. . . ."

They had had a long discussion on the phone one night, and they both agreed that it would be very effective to end the scene with Kimberly lying on the ground, hugging the earth and clutching at the grass, even though it wasn't in the movie or the script for the play.

"But it will look very dramatic on the stage," Veronica had said.

Kimberly stood up, brushed off her skirt, and went through the whole number.

Over the weeks, Kimberly had lost her shyness. She wanted the part very badly and she threw herself into the role with a great deal of energy.

But whenever she opened her mouth to sing, the most awful sounds came out. Kimberly still sang through her nose in a loud monotone. She sang every note the same way, except when she tried to reach high notes. Then she screeched.

Veronica sang the opening number again in the strong, clear voice that had won her the part of Eliza in *My Fair Lady* the year before.

"Now you try it," she said patiently to Kimberly.

"But that's exactly how I *was* singing it," Kimberly protested, but she went through the whole scene again.

This time it sounded even worse.

A young man who was out for a walk in the park came running over to Veronica.

"What's the matter?" he panted. "Should I call the police?"

"No, thank you," Veronica said.

"But I heard these awful screams." He looked over to where Kimberly was lying on the ground, hugging the earth and clutching at the grass. "Is she all right?" the man asked Veronica.

"She's fine," Veronica told him. "We were just rehearsing a play."

When the man had gone, Veronica looked down at Kimberly, who was still holding her pose. She thought how much *she* wanted to play the part of Maria.

But it was too late. She had promised Kimberly she would not even try out. Not only that — Kimberly had made her raise her right hand and swear she would never play the part of Maria in *The Sound of Music* in her whole life!

Veronica was beginning to get worried. There were only four more weeks left before the tryouts.

Four more Saturdays — and Kimberly still did not sing quite as well as Veronica's cat, Gulliver.

". . . *before* I gave him the lessons," she told herself.

Hilary called Veronica that night to bring her up to date on the Children's Committee to Reopen the Harding Branch of the Public Library.

"Melody and I finally thought of a better name," Hilary said. "What do you think of this: Kids for Harding?"

"I'm not sure I like it." Veronica knew that Hilary and Melody were spending a lot of time together working on a plan to get the library opened again. Of course Veronica had been very busy with Kimberly, but she still felt they were trying to save the library behind her back.

"It's certainly not a *great* name," Veronica added.

But Hilary was very excited. "Well, we needed

a name in a hurry! We're going to have a party on Halloween — a letter-raising party! You see, kids will come in costumes, play games, have refreshments — and before they go, we'll make every one of them write a letter to the mayor about how much they need a library again. It was Melody's idea. Isn't it terrific?"

"Sounds like something Melody would think of," Veronica muttered, but she wished she had thought of it. "Besides, I can't even go. I'm not allowed out on Halloween. I'm being punished for the piano."

"You mean no costume — no trick-or-treating?"

"Yup," Veronica said.

"Oh, Veronica! That's awful!" Hilary was quiet for a moment. "Why didn't you tell me?"

"Oh, it's not so bad," Veronica said. "My mother and I are going to my grandfather's in Vermont for Thanksgiving, and of course I'll be going to Santa Barbara for Christmas, anyway. That will make up for it." She paused and thought a moment. "Oh, by the way, Hilary, if Kimberly can't go, do you think you'll be able to?"

Right away Veronica was sorry she had said that. There was a long silence at the other end of the line.

"No, thank you," Hilary said in her most formal voice. "We'll be visiting my cousins in Rhode Island. We do that every Christmas."

"But . . ." Veronica said.

It was too late.

"Well, I just wanted to tell you the news," Hilary said politely, and she hung up.

Veronica sat there for a while, staring at the phone. When her mother returned from her Saturday aerobics class, Veronica asked her for her father's telephone number in Santa Barbara.

Her mother was surprised. "What do you need *that* for?"

"I just wanted to say hello." Veronica did not want to discuss her Christmas plans with her mother — not yet. She wasn't taking any chances with any more holiday punishments. She wanted to get over being punished on Halloween first.

"Your father has an unlisted number," her mother went on. "Even I don't have it. We communicate only through our lawyers. You know that, Veronica." She looked at Veronica.

"What do you want to talk to him about? You remember how upset you got the last time you saw him?"

Veronica vaguely remembered a terrible scene in a lawyer's office when she was much younger. It was something she never wanted to think about.

But, while her mother was in the bathtub, Veronica called the information operator in Santa Barbara, California.

Her mother had told her the truth. Lorenzo Schmidt had an unlisted number, "at the customer's request," the operator told Veronica.

"But I'm sure he would want *me* to have it," Veronica said.

The operator told Veronica she was not allowed to give it out at all. "That's our policy," she said.

Veronica had a terrible week at school. Hilary avoided her completely, and when she gave Kimberly the "Suggested Packing List" of things to bring to Santa Barbara, Kimberly laughed in her face.

"You know, I *have* been there," Kimberly told Veronica. "My aunt lives in Montecito. I know perfectly well what to pack."

It turned out that Kimberly still hadn't remembered to ask her parents if she could go.

The night before Halloween, Veronica took out the card she had received from her father in September along with the California snowman.

She read it to make sure he really wanted her to bring a friend:

Sorry I forgot your birthday. Hope this makes you laugh. Been terribly busy fixing up an old Victorian house. Lots of room. Hope to be settled by the end of November. Your loving Dad.

Veronica read it over and over again. For some reason she couldn't find the part where he invited her to Santa Barbara for Christmas vacation.

# Waiting
# in the Wings

Halloween wasn't quite as bad as Veronica had expected it would be, but of course she never told her mother that.

On Halloween night Veronica had to stay home. She wasn't allowed out. She wasn't even allowed to answer the door when the trick-or-treaters came around. But Mrs. Moore was baby-sitting that evening and so involved in her favorite game show on TV, she never even heard the doorbell.

So Veronica answered the doorbell and, in between, worked on the nun's habit that Kimberly would be wearing for the tryouts — the costume she would toss into the air in the opening number.

Chris and Peter came to her door trick-or-treating three times that evening. Veronica suspected they felt sorry for her. Chris was dressed as a scientist and Peter was The Walking Mummy.

Peter's costume gave Veronica an idea. His head was wrapped in bandages, but his arms stuck straight out in plaster casts painted white.

"We made them ourselves," Chris said. "It took three whole weekends."

"What are they made out of?" Veronica asked curiously.

"Papier-mâché," Chris told her.

"Um . . . Chris?" she said, during their third visit to her door. "Do you think you could design something like that for me? But more like a broken arm cast — a cast I can slip on and off?"

"Well," Chris said, "it wouldn't be easy, but I guess, if we made it a little wide where the elbow turns, you could slip it on and off. What do you want it for?"

"Oh, for next Halloween," Veronica said. "But I need it very soon. I need it the Friday before Thanksgiving vacation."

"So you can practice for next Halloween —right?" Chris seemed to understand.

"Yes," Veronica said.

"Are you sure you want a broken arm costume

for next Halloween?" Chris asked. "It's not all that funny."

"This would be a *serious* costume," Veronica explained.

Chris came back a fourth time that evening to take the measurements of Veronica's right arm.

It was raining and cold on Saturday morning, but Veronica and Kimberly went to their hill in the park, anyway, to practice for the tryouts.

Veronica had lent Kimberly the beautiful boiled wool blue cape that her mother had brought back from Switzerland in September for Veronica. It had edelweiss and red ribbon trimming around the hood and along the front panels.

Veronica just wore her rehearsal clothes with her raincoat over them. But she had tucked a bright pink chiffon scarf into the sleeve so that Kimberly would be able to see her arm while she directed her.

To Veronica's surprise, Kimberly's voice sounded better. At first she thought it was the way it carried in the rain.

"No, it's the chiffon scarf," Kimberly said, when

Veronica told her how much she had improved. "It just seems to help me."

"But Kimberly, you're doing beautifully. You're singing different notes instead of all the same note!" Veronica was very excited. "And some of them are even right!"

There was no question in Veronica's mind that Kimberly would get the part.

"Do you really think so?" Kimberly kept asking.

"I know so," Veronica said.

They rehearsed the scene again and again in the pouring rain. Then they walked through the park with their arms around each other.

When they got to the edge of the park, Kimberly said, "You know, Veronica, today would be a good day to break your arm. It's very slippery and — what if you fell out of a tree or something?"

"Kimberly," Veronica said, "everything is under control."

Throughout the month of November Kimberly's voice got better and better. Every once in a while Veronica wondered if, perhaps, her own ears had changed, but, after a while, there was no question about it: Kimberly was definitely hitting different notes.

"Now, if you could try to sing a little less through your nose . . ." Veronica coached her.

The tryouts were Monday afternoon after school the week before Thanksgiving vacation.

That morning Veronica stepped off the bus with the cast Chris and Peter had made for her on her right arm.

She had put it on during the bus ride, along with the sling that held it. And, in her pocket, she carried the note she had written from her doctor explaining that Veronica would be unable to try out for the part of Maria. She would be in a cast for months. It was a very serious break.

She couldn't wait for Kimberly to see her. To her surprise, Kimberly was waiting at the top of the school steps, wearing the nun's habit Veronica had designed.

Kimberly gasped. "Veronica!" she said. "How did you do it? How did you break your arm?"

"I'd rather not talk about it," Veronica said.

Kimberly was a little hurt. She wanted to know

if Veronica had used any of *her* ideas. But she spent the rest of the day protecting Veronica's arm in the hallways so no one would bump into it.

"It hurts a lot, right?" Kimberly asked.

"It's a bit painful," Veronica admitted.

Right before the tryouts Kimberly took Veronica backstage. Miss Levy was practicing the piano on the stage. She had been very distressed when she saw Veronica's broken arm and the note from the doctor.

"Veronica," Kimberly said, "I have a surprise for you," and she pulled off her nun's habit.

Veronica couldn't believe her eyes. Kimberly had had her hair all cut off.

"Just like Maria," Veronica said weakly. She thought Kimberly looked a bit odd in that haircut. Her face was too long or something.

"I know," Kimberly said.

She was very confident about getting the part.

"Where's the pink scarf?" Kimberly asked.

"I left it home!" Veronica said.

"What?" Kimberly was very upset.

"I can't wear it, anyway," Veronica explained. "Look, I have a cast on that arm."

"I don't get it," Kimberly said in a dull voice. "How are you going to direct me?"

"With my left arm, I guess." Veronica felt terrible. She was sure someone would notice if she switched the cast now. Besides, Chris and Peter had designed it so well, it probably could only be worn on the right arm.

"Why couldn't you have broken the other arm?" Kimberly asked crossly.

Veronica was sure that, if Kimberly did not get the part, she would blame Veronica — for forgetting the pink chiffon scarf.

Veronica sat on a stool in the wings right behind the curtains during the tryouts.

Since Kimberly was the only one now trying out for the part of Maria, she would be last.

The seats in the auditorium were filled with fourth-, fifth-, and sixth-graders who were permitted to watch the tryouts.

A hush fell over the audience when Miss Levy began playing the opening number of *The Sound of Music*. Kimberly rushed out onto the stage. Veronica directed her from the side and was pleased that she had thought of making Kimberly hug imaginary trees as well as real ones. There was no scenery for the tryouts.

But something was wrong. Kimberly's voice sounded terrible!

When, at last, Kimberly was lying on the stage pretending to hug the earth and clutch the grass, Veronica jumped off her stool.

She ran over to Miss Levy, who had stopped playing the piano and was staring at Kimberly.

"I know what's wrong!" Veronica shouted. "Start all over again. You're playing in the wrong key. She can really sing it perfectly, but in a different key. I just don't know what one."

Veronica began to sing, "The hills are al-i-ive with the sound of music."

Now Miss Levy was no longer staring at Kimberly. She was staring at Veronica, who was waving her cast around as she sang.

"Veronica, please take your seat," Miss Levy said quietly.

Veronica went back to the stool and peeked out over the footlights. She wondered if Kimberly had been as bad as she thought.

Many of the kids were laughing so hard, they were falling off their seats. Others were just holding their hands over their mouths, trying *not* to laugh.

Amy was sitting very straight with a smile on her face — a smile that said, "I told you so."

But the worse sight of all was Hilary. Hilary was sitting over to the side with tears streaming down her face.

Veronica knew that Hilary was crying — not for Kimberly, but for her.

When Kimberly finally raised her head and looked out over the footlights, she jumped to her feet. For a few seconds she just stood there, frozen. Then she fled.

For a few hours no one could find Kimberly. Around dinnertime they found her hiding behind the lockers in the gym.

Kimberly did not come to school the next day . . .

. . . or the next.

Veronica was called into the headmaster's office. Wingate Craven was "most distressed" about the entire situation and insisted that Veronica try out that afternoon for the part of Maria. "Not only for your sake, Veronica, but for the sake of the school . . ." he said.

"I promised Kimberly I wouldn't," Veronica said.

"I'm afraid your mother and I will have to have a little chat," Mr. Craven said.

Wednesday was a half day of school. It was the day before Thanksgiving. That morning Amy had news of Kimberly:

"She told her mother she's never coming back," Amy announced. "She won't even get out of bed. Her mother told me that all Kimberly will say is that Veronica ruined her life."

Veronica knew it was true. She had ruined Kimberly's life.

# No Stuffing

Veronica's mother was waiting outside the school for her at noon. She had double-parked.

"I didn't want to waste any time," she told Veronica. "I was hoping to beat the Thanksgiving traffic."

They drove in silence to Veronica's grandfather's house in Vermont. When they were on the New England Thruway, Veronica's mother said, "What do you think Wingate wants to see me about? Are you having problems at school? I don't understand. Your marks were excellent this term."

"I don't know." Veronica was looking forward to a nice, peaceful Thanksgiving vacation.

"Maybe it's about fund-raising for the school," her mother said thoughtfully.

"Maybe," Veronica said. If Kimberly wasn't

coming back to school, the school would lose a lot of money. Her father gave large sums of money to Maxton every year.

"Well, what can it be, Veronica? He wanted me to come in this afternoon, but I told him it was impossible. I have to admit Monday isn't a great day for me, either."

"I *am* having problems in soccer," Veronica suggested.

"That surprises me," her mother said. "I was quite good at both field hockey and soccer." She glanced over at Veronica. "Do you want to talk about it?" she asked.

Veronica began talking about her soccer problems. "One time I scored a whole lot of goals, but more than half of them were for the wrong side."

They made good time on the drive to Vermont, and spent the weekend at her grandfather's house.

Her grandfather was a retired country doctor who also believed in staying young. He had strong ideas about physical fitness and health. They had a dietetic Thanksgiving dinner.

No stuffing in the turkey, Veronica thought miserably.

Veronica spent the weekend lying on the couch

in front of the fireplace rereading *How To Win Friends and Influence People*. She was trying to find out what she had done wrong, but there were no clues in the book.

"What in the world are you reading *that* for?" her mother laughed. "Veronica, don't you think you might make an effort to be a little more sociable? And please don't sulk like that. When you do, you actually *create* unattractive lines in your face for the rest of your life."

But Veronica had trouble trying to take an interest in the conversation her mother and grandfather were having about "salt intake."

On the way back home, her mother said, "Veronica, I wanted to talk to you about Christmas plans."

For a moment Veronica's hopes were raised. Maybe she was going to Santa Barbara after all.

"I want to spend a nice, cozy Christmas with you this year," her mother went on. "I have decided to give up my holiday skiing trip."

Veronica's mother usually went skiing in Sun Valley during the week between Christmas and New Year's.

". . . so I'll be leaving for Sun Valley *next* week

for three weeks, and I'll be back on the twenty-first of December so we can have a nice, cozy Christmas together."

"Okay," Veronica said in her most cheerful voice.

A few minutes later her mother said, "Now, while I'm away I want you to clean your room — really clean it, and don't make too much work for Mrs. Moore. We will be having a lovely couple staying with us over the holidays — a German couple I met this summer in Switzerland."

"I don't want a bunch of foreigners hanging around for Christmas!" Veronica protested.

"Why, Veronica!" Her mother was shocked. She spent the next half hour lecturing Veronica on becoming a little more worldly.

Veronica suddenly interrupted. "Mommy," she said. "I mean, Elaine, I have to ask you something."

"Just a minute. I have to find the turn-off," her mother said.

"Something serious," Veronica added.

"I will be able to listen a lot better when I get to the turn-off," her mother said patiently.

When they finally had turned onto the thruway, Veronica said, "Did Daddy leave us because I was

". . . um . . . more trouble than I'm worth?"

Her mother was quiet for a while. Veronica knew she didn't like to talk about her father or the divorce. Finally she said, "First of all, your father did not leave *us*. Our marriage was simply not working out for a long time before the divorce. We came from different worlds."

Just then the line of traffic stopped up ahead and her mother put her foot on the brake. "Now what?" Elaine Schmidt groaned.

Veronica saw flashing lights up ahead. She had the feeling that her mother had only answered part of her question, but her mother was getting very irritable. The line of traffic was moving very slowly.

"Oh, honestly," her mother suddenly said, "it's an accident. Veronica, cover your eyes!"

Veronica covered her eyes. Her mother always made her do that. Veronica hated it. She was sure she was picturing something much worse than anything she could ever see. Besides, she had watched all sorts of highway shows with Mrs. Moore — shows full of car crashes and stretchers, not to mention the evening news.

"Mommy . . ." Veronica began.

"Veronica! I said cover your eyes. You know how upset you get."

"No, I don't," Veronica said, but she covered her eyes.

Veronica's imagination was running wild with all kinds of grisly scenes. When she heard her mother say, "We'll make up the time on the Connecticut Turnpike," Veronica knew they had passed the scene of the accident. But she was still thinking terrible thoughts. She tried to think of something more pleasant.

"Mommy," she said suddenly. "What did I do in that lawyer's office — the last time I saw Daddy? Why do you always say I got so upset?"

"Oh, Veronica, you must remember. It was only three summers ago."

"I don't remember," Veronica said. "Tell me. *Tell me now.*"

Her mother sighed. "You just don't *want* to remember how you behaved. I have to admit it was probably a mistake when I took you to Malcolm's law office. Especially since you hadn't seen your father for so long."

"Go on," Veronica said. "What did I do?"

"All of a sudden you started shrieking like a

banshee. No one could understand a word you said. Then you started kicking and punching Lorenzo — your own father! You grabbed Malcolm around the neck and almost strangled him. We had to use physical force to get you to let go!"

They were getting close to the city.

"To make a long story short," her mother went on, "since no one could figure out what your father had done to make you so upset, we decided it would be best for you not to see him — that he was not to contact you, except by mail."

When her mother returned from her appointment with Wingate Craven Monday afternoon, she told Veronica she simply *had* to try out for the part of Maria.

"I promised Kimberly I wouldn't," Veronica said.

"I'm sure Kimberly doesn't care anymore," her mother said. "Besides, apparently you also promised Miss Levy you *would* try out."

"I did not promise Miss Levy I would try out," Veronica said. "I promised her I would *sign up*."

"Did you tell Wingate that?" her mother asked.

"Yes," Veronica said.

Her mother laughed. "I must confess that bro-

111

ken arm episode makes me laugh. Naturally I did not let Wingate know I was amused."

Veronica did not see what was so funny.

Later when her mother was busy packing for her ski trip, Veronica asked, "What's my punishment?"

Her mother sighed. "Veronica, you're standing right in my way."

Veronica moved aside so her mother could get to the clothes closet.

"What's my punishment?" Veronica asked again.

"To tell you the truth, I'm too busy packing right now to think about it. Besides, I want to give it some thought."

Veronica was furious. "While you're skiing?" she asked. "Can't you tell me now?"

"Veronica," her mother said quietly, "first of all, I don't like your tone, and secondly, you're standing right in my way again."

The following week, a sign was posted in the lunchroom: "The production of *The Sound of Music* has been canceled."

On a Thursday afternoon while her mother was away, Veronica decided to take Lady Jane Grey on a nice long walk. She ended up sitting on the steps of the Harding Branch of the public library. A sign on the door said: CLOSED UNTIL FURTHER NOTICE.

She thought about the good old days when Hilary was still her friend and they used to come to the library together to help Miss Markham, the children's librarian.

Just then she saw Miss Markham coming toward her on the sidewalk.

Veronica wanted to hide. She was embarrassed for Miss Markham's sake that Miss Markham was now unemployed. When the library had closed, she had been laid off, or "excessed," as the newspapers had said.

But Miss Markham did not seem embarrassed at all. In fact she seemed delighted to see Veronica.

"I missed you at the Halloween letter-raising party," Miss Markham said.

"Oh," Veronica said. "How was it?"

"Didn't Hilary tell you about it?" Miss Markham asked.

"We . . . um . . . haven't exactly been in touch," Veronica said sadly.

"I am sorry to hear that," Miss Markham said.

"Well, I'm afraid the party was a disaster. Everyone had a wonderful time, of course, but no one wrote a single letter to the mayor. 'Later. Later,' they kept saying. Melody ended up screaming at the kids and Hilary, to my surprise, tried to drag them over to the letter-writing table."

The party had been a failure. Veronica was surprised that she didn't feel good about that. She felt terrible.

There was something she wanted desperately to ask Miss Markham. "Let's say," she began, "you're doing this research. Let's say you're trying to find someone and that person has an unlisted number and a post office box. Do you think the library could help you find him?"

"Sounds like it would be quite a piece of detective work," Miss Markham said slowly, "but I guess if you knew what kind of work this person did, you might find some sort of directory — "

"Oh, thank you, Miss Markham!" Veronica shouted. She didn't want to take up any more of Miss Markham's time. After all, Miss Markham wasn't being paid to be a librarian anymore.

"Good luck, Veronica!" Miss Markham called after her.

114

Veronica picked up Lady Jane Grey and ran all the way home. She got on the phone and called Santa Barbara information. She got the number of the Santa Barbara Public Library and called.

"Santa Barbara Public Library, Central Branch," said a voice.

"Hello," Veronica said. "I'm doing some research — "

"Hold on a minute." Before Veronica could say anything, she was switched to the central children's room. Veronica was slightly insulted that they assumed she was a child.

"Central Children's Room. Peggy Stark speaking."

Veronica began. "You see, I'm doing some research and I wanted to know if there was a Directory of Businessmen in Santa Barbara. My name is Veronica Schmidt and I am calling long distance."

"Veronica Schmidt?" the librarian asked.

"Yes," Veronica said.

"*The* Veronica Schmidt?" The librarian sounded very excited.

Veronica thought she might be dreaming.

"You're quite a celebrity here," Peggy Stark went

115

on. "We have that letter you wrote to the news-paper up on our bulletin board — the letter you wrote about the closing of your local library. We've had it on the bulletin board for almost a year. Your father brought it in. He wanted me to see it. Your father is sure proud of *you!*"

Veronica was so surprised, she didn't know what to say. "I know," she finally said. "Um . . . do you see him often?"

"He stops by here all the time to make sure that letter is still up there."

"Um . . . do you think you could tell him to give me a ring?" Veronica asked. "I need some ad-vice from him. It isn't an emergency exactly, but. . . ."

"I'll stop by the boatyard after work and tell him you're trying to reach him," the librarian said.

"Thank you." Veronica was pleased to hear that her father owned a boat.

When she had hung up, she danced around the house for a few hours with her fingers in her ears so she wouldn't have to listen to the TV set. Mrs. Moore didn't even notice.

At eight o'clock a person-to-person call came in to Veronica Schmidt.

"This is Veronica Schmidt," Veronica said.

"Veronica, this is Daddy."

"Oh Daddy, I'm so happy you called." Veronica's voice was trembling. "Tell me something. What do you do when you've ruined somebody's life?"

"Shh, shh, baby," her father said softly. "Start at the beginning."

# Veronica Goes West

No one had ever talked to Veronica like that.

But what surprised her the most was that her father's voice wasn't anything like Dwayne Cutler's. He didn't have a low, deep voice; he had a slow, gentle way of speaking and a real Western drawl.

Veronica tried to start at the beginning. She tried to tell the story step-by-step in a nice orderly way. She had a feeling she wasn't doing a very good job when her father said he didn't quite understand the part where she was giving Kimberly singing lessons and the piano came through the window and broke her arm.

Veronica thought for a moment. Finally, she asked, "Do you mind if I start at the end?"

118

"Not at all," her father said gently. "Now that I think of it, the end is probably a much better place to start."

"You see, Kimberly trusted me. Oh Daddy, she trusted me so much!" Veronica thought of that trust. Suddenly she saw Kimberly lying on the stage, clutching imaginary grass.

Veronica began to cry.

"Oh Daddy," Veronica sobbed. "I don't mean . . . to . . . be . . . crying . . . long distance. It must be . . . terribly . . . expensive." But she couldn't stop herself.

"Don't worry about that," her father said. "I just want to know if you can cry and listen at the same time."

"Yes," Veronica said, and she tried to cry a little more softly.

"It's hard to talk about this over the phone," her father said. "Listen to me, Veronica. I want you to come out here for Christmas vacation. The house isn't finished yet, but I'll get you a room at the Old Yacht Club Inn. I'm calling your mother's lawyer right away, and I'm sending you a plane ticket . . . are you still there?"

"I'm here," Veronica said. "I stopped crying."

"Well, would you like to come?" her father asked.

"Would I like to come?" Veronica shouted. "Why do you think I invited myself in that letter?"

"What letter?" her father asked.

"That letter I sent you — thanking you for the California snowman!"

"I never got that letter," her father said.

"Thank you very much for the snowman," Veronica said politely. "It was very funny."

"I don't understand it," her father said.

"Neither do I!" Veronica burst out. "I guess I'm not very good at jokes." She had spent the last few months trying to figure out when exactly that snowman had melted.

"Not the snowman," her father said. "The letter. I don't understand why I didn't get your letter."

But it no longer mattered. In fact Veronica felt slightly embarrassed about that letter. And now she had a real invitation to Santa Barbara.

Late that night her mother called from Sun Valley to give her permission ". . . just as long as we have our cozy little Christmas together. The von Kronbergs are coming all the way from Europe. It would be a shame if they didn't catch a glimpse of you. You can go the next day."

120

On Christmas Day, Veronica was so charming to their European house guests, she had a feeling her mother was slightly relieved when she excused herself to go across the hall to see Chris. She brought him the menus she had prepared for Gulliver and Lady Jane Grey and ran through the list of games that her cat and dog enjoyed.

"I don't want them to suffer while I'm away," Veronica explained and was pleased when Chris studied the games carefully and asked questions about them.

The next day her mother drove her to the airport. "Promise me you won't get yourself upset the way you did the last time you saw your father."

Veronica promised.

Veronica boarded the plane for Los Angeles. She had never been so excited in her life. She was going to California "maybe forever," she told herself, "to start life anew, become a different person — a quiet unassuming person who always tells the truth," she decided.

The stewardess on her flight was named Lillian and she was very nice.

"My name is Veronica," she told her, "but most of my friends call me Ronnie — actually they call me Rhonda." To Veronica the name Rhonda really sounded "California."

They landed at Los Angeles International Airport at one o'clock Pacific Time. Veronica followed Lillian through the long corridors of Los Angeles Airport on the way to the baggage claim.

"I'll wait with you," Lillian told her. "I want to make sure your father meets you."

To Veronica's surprise people passing by smiled at her and said, "Hello" and "Hi, there!" Veronica ran to catch up to Lillian.

"How do they know me?" she whispered. "A whole bunch of people just said hello."

The stewardess smiled. "They're just being friendly. Remember, Rhonda, you're in California!"

From then on Veronica said hello to every single person they passed.

"Do you see your father anywhere?" Lillian asked as Veronica waited for her suitcase to come around on the carousel.

Veronica searched the crowd outside the gate. There was only one man dressed in a business suit. She nodded.

When she finally got her bag, she dragged it

over to the man. It was quite a heavy bag. Veronica had brought tins of food, a canteen for water, a flashlight, a transistor radio, and enough batteries to last a few weeks in addition to all her clothes. She had prepared herself for an earthquake exactly the way her pamphlet WHAT TO DO IF AN EARTHQUAKE STRIKES had suggested.

"Hi, Daddy," Veronica said. "I'm here."

The man stared down at her in surprise.

Someone else was tugging at her suitcase trying to pull it away from her. She looked up and saw a tall slim man with sandy blond hair. He was dressed in a white T-shirt with a soft suede jacket over it. He was wearing jeans and cowboy boots.

He was nice-looking and had a very friendly face, but Veronica held onto her suitcase and wouldn't let go.

"I'm Daddy," the man said. "Don't you remember me?"

Veronica looked at him thoughtfully.

"Yes, I do," she said slowly, "but the last time I saw you, you were wearing a suit, and the last time I saw you, *you were the lawyer*."

Veronica felt her face turn bright red. She stared down at the ground.

Her father was quiet for a moment.

"Do you think you got us mixed up?" he asked. "Did you get me and Mommy's lawyer mixed up?"

Veronica nodded. She didn't trust herself to speak, and she was afraid to look up.

Suddenly she was lifted into the air and swung around and around. Then she held very still and let herself be hugged.

"Oh Veronica," the tall cowboy whispered, "if you only knew how much I've missed you."

# Candy

The drive up the coast was beautiful. At first Veronica didn't know what to say.

"Well, Daddy," she began, "what have you been up to?"

"I've been quite lucky in the last few years," he told her. "I designed a boat — not a pleasure boat, a work boat, but it became quite popular up and down the coast. With the money I made from that I bought the boatyard in Santa Barbara where all the repairs are done."

"And all this time I thought you were a businessman," Veronica said.

"I *am* a businessman," her father said.

"But you don't look like one," Veronica said. "You look more like a country-western singer."

Her father laughed. "Well, strangely enough, a

few years ago I had my own band. Do you like country music?"

"Oh yes!" Veronica said. "Mrs. Moore and I watch *Country Jamboree* every Saturday night."

Veronica found herself telling her father the whole story about Kimberly. "I thought I would be able to teach her to sing because I had been very successful with Gulliver. Gulliver is my cat."

"*Your* cat?" her father laughed. "So Gulliver is still around?"

Veronica was surprised. "You know Gulliver?"

"Gulliver was my cat before I got married. I found Gulliver one snowy night when he was just a kitten hiding behind a garbage can in an alley in Buffalo, New York."

Gulliver was an alley cat? Veronica was horrified. "But Daddy, I've spent my whole life telling everyone that Gulliver was a pure pedigree — half Persian, half Siamese, half Angora and half Calico!"

"I wonder why you thought that," her father said.

Veronica didn't say anything. She was pretty sure she had heard it from her mother.

"Anyway," she went on, "I promised Kimberly

I wouldn't try out, and I only promised Miss Levy that I would *sign up* to try out. I did not promise her I would actually try out."

"But you weren't planning to try out, were you? It sounds as if you made a promise to Miss Levy in bad faith," her father said.

Veronica had never heard that expression before, but she had a feeling she knew what it meant. She looked at her father. He didn't seem angry at her, but she was pretty sure he was the sort of person who never told lies — "Like Hilary," Veronica thought.

She decided right then she would never tell another lie.

"Do you like bicycle riding?" her father asked.

"Oh yes!" Veronica said before she could stop herself.

"Terrific!" her father said. "There are bicycles at the inn, and it's an easy ride to the boatyard. You can visit me there whenever you feel like it. Santa Barbara is made for bicycle riding."

Veronica didn't think this was the time to tell her father she had never ridden a bicycle in her life. Maybe she could learn in a hurry.

"But I'm going to have the house ready when

127

you come out for spring vacation," her father said.

Veronica stared at him in amazement. "But you haven't even had me for Christmas vacation yet. How do you know you're going to be able to *put up with me*?"

"What makes you say that?" her father asked.

"Daddy," Veronica said, "you don't even know what you're *getting*. Most people think I'm more trouble than I'm worth."

"How much are you worth?" her father asked.

Veronica giggled. "More trouble than I'm."

"You're worth more than anything in the world to me," her father said quietly.


Santa Barbara was the most beautiful town Veronica had ever seen. It was set between the mountains and the sea. There were large old trees lining State Street and adobe brick buildings with red tile roofs. Everything looked so clean!

Her father took her to the library to introduce her to Peggy Stark.

"Welcome to Santa Barbara," the librarian said. "Eva has been waiting to meet you." She introduced Veronica to a very pretty girl with blonde, almost white, hair pulled back in a pony tail. "Eva is thirteen. She helps out in the children's room after school."

Veronica was surprised that a girl who was thirteen wanted to meet her.

"I was about to get Veronica some ice cream at Hobson's," her father told Eva.

"Oh yes." Eva seemed very sure of herself. "She would enjoy that. Hobson's ice cream is very popular with the younger generation."

"Would you like to come, too?" Veronica's father asked Eva.

Veronica was afraid Eva would be insulted to be invited along on such a babyish treat, but Eva just shrugged and said, "Sure."

At first Veronica thought Eva was just going along to be nice, but, once they got to the ice cream parlor, Eva seemed very familiar with Hobson's. "The *only* kind to have," she explained to Veronica, "is cream and caramel with Junior Mints mixed in."

They stood in the shade on the sidewalk eating their ice cream and talking. "Your library still isn't open?" Eva was shocked. "After that letter you wrote to the newspaper. That's so cold!"

Veronica guessed that the expression, "That's

so cold," was California for "How awful!" She told Eva about the party to raise letters that Hilary and Melody had given.

"Well, of course it didn't work," Eva said at once. "They should have made the kids write letters *before* they let them in the door. You know, dangle the refreshments in front of their greedy little eyes. . . ."

Veronica was so impressed with Eva's suggestion, she immediately gave Eva Hilary's address so she could write to her. She didn't want to mention the fact that she and Hilary were no longer friends.

Then Eva wrote her own name and telephone number for Veronica. Veronica stared at the slip of paper. Eva signed her name Eva Wright. Veronica thought it was very sophisticated of Eva to dot the "i" with a heart.

"I love hearts," Eva said. Veronica noticed that Eva had earrings with hearts and a chain around her neck with a heart on it, too.

"Call me tonight," Eva said. "You can bike down to the library tomorrow and I'll show you around."

"Sure," Veronica said, "um . . . unless my father has made other plans."

Her father took her to the Old Yacht Club Inn. Veronica loved it. It looked just like a gingerbread house. There was a lemon tree in the front yard.

After she had unpacked, he took her to the bicycle shed in back and Veronica chose a yellow racing bike.

"Don't you want to try it out?" her father asked.

Veronica had been waiting for just the right moment to tell her father she couldn't ride, but, to her horror, she heard herself say, "I'm sure it will be all right. It's exactly like the one I have at home."

They sat on the front porch and her father went over the bicycle map of Santa Barbara with Veronica. "Many of the streets have lanes just for bicycles," he explained, and he marked the path that led along the beach to the boatyard. "The main streets here go east and west, but there's a trick to Santa Barbara. . . ."

Veronica was having trouble paying attention. She was wondering what would happen if there was an earthquake tomorrow. Would they close off the streets? Would they forbid all bicycle-riding?

She heard her father say, "Of course, if you like,

131

I could call Candy and see if she's free tomorrow. She could drive you around and show you the sights. Then she could drop you at the boatyard."

"What a good idea!" Veronica said. She did not particularly want her father to have to hire a baby-sitter for her, but what else could she do?

Veronica sat on the porch of the inn the next morning and waited. Her baby-sitter was late.

The leaves of the lemon tree were glistening with raindrops from an early morning shower. Veronica tried to see into the ivy that grew in the garden. She checked to make sure she had her pamphlet HOW TO AVOID A RATTLESNAKE BITE in the heavy knapsack she called her Earthquake Safety Kit.

Right before noon a shiny turquoise-blue sports convertible pulled up in front of the inn, and a slim young woman stepped out.

She was wearing faded jeans, an over-sized sweater, and tennis shoes. Her blonde hair was cut all jagged, but it looked wonderfully wind-blown and casual. "California perfect!" Veronica thought.

The young woman waved to Veronica. "Hi,

Veronica!" she called. "What are you waiting for?" And, in one graceful motion, she was back in the sports car.

Veronica couldn't believe it.

She ran down the path to the car.

"Are you Candy?" she asked.

"I sure am," the woman said. "Hop in!"

Veronica couldn't move. She just stared at the woman. Candy looked like a Barbie-doll — only much prettier.

She's nothing like Mrs. Moore! Veronica thought. Baby-sitters sure are different in California!

# Veronica Chills Out

Veronica got into the car.

"What kind of car is this?" she asked Candy.

Candy flashed her a dimpled smile. "It's a Karmann Ghia. Do you like it?"

"It's fantastic!" Veronica said. "Is it yours?"

Candy laughed. "It sure is."

Veronica figured baby-sitters must do a lot better in California.

She put her sunglasses on top of her head (Candy wore hers like that), and she draped her arm on the door the way Candy did.

"What's in there?" Candy asked, pointing to the knapsack on Veronica's lap.

"Oh, just a few things — you know, suntan lotion . . ." Veronica felt a bit shy admitting that she had enough tin cans of food and water to last three days in the event of an earthquake. She also had enough batteries to keep the flashlight and radio going for a few weeks.

"Well, sling it in the back," Candy said.

Veronica did as she was told, and Candy started the motor.

"I'm sorry I'm so late," Candy said as they drove along. "We had a puppy shower this morning."

At first Veronica didn't know what Candy meant. Then she remembered the early morning rainstorm.

"Oh yes," Veronica said. "I noticed it, too, but back East we call it 'raining cats and dogs.' "

"What?" Candy asked.

"I said, 'Back East we call it raining cats and dogs,' " Veronica explained.

Candy burst out laughing. Veronica felt slightly ridiculous when she learned that Candy had a small business called Parties for Pets.

"When a dog is expecting puppies, we are hired to give a party — like a baby shower. The expectant mother is registered at the pet store — you know, the owners sign up for gifts for the mother and the puppies."

"Then you arrange the parties and other dogs

come to them?" Veronica asked. She now understood that Candy didn't make *all* her money babysitting.

"You got it," Candy said. "Look, the zoo is right near here. I'll take you there first."

"The zoo?" Veronica laughed to show how silly she thought zoos were. "I'm a bit old for the zoo!" She was hoping to impress her cool baby-sitter.

Candy's light blue eyes were like the glass eyes of a China doll. Veronica had the feeling she was annoyed, but she flashed that dimpled smile again and said, "Then why don't we just drive down the coast a bit."

They drove for a while, past a bird refuge and along Butterfly Beach in Montecito. Then Candy drove Veronica around to a few shopping malls, and Veronica followed Candy in and out of fancy shops. Candy took Veronica to have her hair cut just like hers and out for lunch at a Mexican restaurant in a patio in the middle of Santa Barbara.

Veronica sat at the table swinging her hair around to make sure it fell into place the way Candy's did.

"After lunch will you drop me off at the boatyard?" she asked Candy. It was already 2:30.

"Don't be silly," Candy said. "Your father has enough work. You'll just be in his way. And he spends all his spare time on that house." She laughed. "You certainly didn't pick the most convenient time to show up."

Veronica felt very nervous. "But he invited me to the boatyard. He wants me to come."

Candy was looking at her watch. "The service sure is slow here," she muttered.

"He said you'd drop me off there," Veronica said.

"Relax," Candy said. "We'll see."

After they had eaten, Candy stopped at the post office to pick up Veronica's father's mail. When she got back in the car, she held one of the letters up to the sunlight and tried to read through the envelope.

She saw Veronica watching her. "I like to screen out the junk mail," she told Veronica. "Your father has enough on his mind."

"I want to go to the boatyard." Veronica's voice had gotten quite loud. "I want to go to the boatyard *right now*. Daddy wants me to come."

"Oh Veronica," Candy said in disgust, "chill out!"

Veronica hadn't the faintest idea what that meant, but it scared her. She was quiet when they stopped in front of an old Victorian house on the corner of De la Vina Street. It was painted pink with gray trim.

Candy handed Veronica the letters. "Be a good girl and drop these into your father's mailbox."

Veronica stared up at the beautiful old house. This was the house her father was renovating.

She took the letters and got out of the car. She went up the steps to the big wooden porch and dropped the letters into the mailbox.

Veronica looked back at Candy, who was sitting in the car reading something. She was convulsed with laughter. Since Candy seemed to be having so much fun, Veronica figured she had a little time to look through the windows and take a peek at the garden on the side of the house. The garden was overgrown, but Veronica was delighted. She would help her father with that garden over spring vacation.

She walked back to the car. Candy was still reading. When Veronica saw what was amusing Candy so much, she froze.

Candy was reading her pamphlet WHAT TO DO IF AN EARTHQUAKE STRIKES. And her Earthquake Safety Kit had been opened!

"You're unbelievable!" Candy said when she saw Veronica staring at her. "And you've got a better supply of batteries than the California National Guard!"

"It's not funny," Veronica said. "How dare you go through my things?"

But Candy found the whole thing terribly amusing.

"So you're still dreaming about earthquakes?" she said. "Well, better safe than sorry," and she burst out laughing again.

Veronica waited until Candy had stopped laughing.

"How did you know I dreamed about earthquakes?" Veronica asked quietly.

Candy shrugged. "Hop in," she said. "Look, I've got to get home. I'm expecting a phone call. We can hang out there for a while — watch a little TV."

Veronica repeated the question. "How did you know I dreamed about earthquakes?"

Candy looked at her watch. "Don't be a drag," she said, tapping her fingernails on the steering wheel. "Hop in."

"You opened that letter I wrote to my father,"

Veronica said, "but he never even saw it. The dream was in that letter!"

Suddenly Candy flashed the most brilliant smile Veronica had ever seen. It was dazzling!

"Look, honey," Candy said, "if you're so anxious to go to the boatyard, why don't you just take the bicycle in your father's garage. You just go straight down De la Vina Street to get to the boatyard."

Veronica stared at Candy.

Candy sighed and climbed out of the car. She went to the garage and returned with a red bicycle.

Veronica took the bicycle from Candy and let Candy help her get the knapsack on her back.

"It's 4:30," Candy said. "You'd better get going. Do you have a map?"

Veronica nodded. The map was in her knapsack.

Candy got back into the turquoise-blue sports car and drove off.

"Later!" she called over her shoulder.

Veronica watched the car speed off. She didn't know what "later" meant, but she knew she'd been dismissed.

# The Sun Sets West

Veronica walked quickly down De la Vina Street wheeling the bicycle along on the sidewalk. She walked for twenty minutes enjoying the freedom, the smell of the eucalyptus trees, and the lovely gardens around the houses. Her knapsack full of survival gear was very heavy, but it made her feel secure to know that, if worse came to worst, she had three days to get to the boatyard.

She knew her father would be worried that it was taking her longer than it should, but she also knew he would wait for her at the boatyard. And he would understand at once when she confessed she couldn't ride a bicycle and had to walk.

She also knew she was heading west toward the ocean because she was going in the direction of the setting sun. That puzzled her a bit since it was much too early for the sun to set.

After all, it was summertime in Santa Barbara, and Veronica knew that, in the summer, there would be daylight until eight or nine o'clock. "The sun only *seems* to be setting," Veronica told herself.

But the sun continued to go down. Veronica knew she must be getting near the harbor, but she decided to check her map.

She studied the street sign of the road that crossed De la Vina. Then she laid her bicycle on the grass and sat down on the curb to look at her map.

Veronica gasped. For the last twenty minutes she had been walking in the wrong direction — *away* from the harbor, but toward the setting sun.

That meant the sun was setting in the wrong place. It was setting in the east! But the sun wasn't supposed to be setting at all — not for a few hours at least!

Veronica had gotten the highest marks in Earth Science, which she had studied in the third grade. "If *I* can't figure this out," she told herself calmly, "no one can."

She took a deep breath and began talking out loud to herself. There were no people around anyway — just a few cars.

"Now," she began, "the sun probably knows what it's doing. Therefore it is *not* summertime here; it only feels like summer." Suddenly she realized she had hit on the truth. Santa Barbara was far above the equator. It was wintertime.

"The sun was right to set!" Veronica shouted.

Her mind began to clear and she worked on the next problem. "So," she said, "we have a choice: Either the sun set in the wrong place or the Pacific Ocean is in the wrong place."

It didn't sound like much of a choice. But Veronica found it helped to talk out loud, so she went on. "Most likely the sun was around before the Pacific Ocean, so the sun knows what it is doing, and the Pacific Ocean is the one that's in the wrong place." Suddenly she remembered her father's words, ". . . but there's a trick to Santa Barbara. . . ."

It was now so dark, Veronica had to use her flashlight to read the map. But in no time at all, she had figured out the "trick." Santa Barbara was on a peninsula. It was on a stretch of the coastline that curved around so much, the harbor and boat-yard were actually to the east!

Veronica took off and began running with the bicycle in the direction from which she had come. When she passed her father's house, she began running faster. Just then her bicycle hit a crack in the sidewalk, fell over and Veronica tumbled into the bicycle.

For a few minutes she just lay there. She was exhausted. Slowly, she untangled herself from the bicycle and wheeled it to her father's front porch. She sat on the step nursing her bruises and cuts with the first-aid kit she had in her knapsack.

It was quite chilly sitting there in the dark, so Veronica took out her heavy sweater and put it on. Then she just sat — too tired to think.

She heard a voice — a soft comforting voice — her father's voice.

"I was hoping I'd find you here," he said.

Veronica looked up at her father.

"Daddy," she said in defeat. "First of all, I can't ride a bicycle. Second of all, the sun set in the right place, the Pacific Ocean was in the right place — *I* was the one who was in the wrong place!"

"So you made the right decision," her father said quietly. "You came home."

Veronica looked around at the beautiful old porch — *her* porch. "Yes," she whispered. "I came home."

Veronica learned to ride a bicycle in two hours and thirty-five minutes.

"It's much easier at your age," her father said, "and it was very nice of you to wait for *me* to give you the lessons."

"You're a very good teacher," Veronica said, and her father looked pleased.

She had to practice for a few days before her father allowed her to ride to the boatyard.

Those days in Santa Barbara were the happiest days of Veronica's life. In the mornings she'd ride along the beach to the boatyard. Her father seemed to enjoy having her around.

Sometimes she even helped. "Watch my truck," a man would say, "I've got to talk to Lorenzo," and Veronica would guard that truck with her life.

In the afternoons she rode to the library and met Eva. They bicycled to the beach, where they would fly kites or build sandcastles. Some kids showed Veronica how to ride a small surfboard called a skim board and Veronica skated around on the wet sand. That was what you did with a skim board.

When it was cloudy, Veronica and Eva curled up on the window seat in Veronica's room and talked. They also spent quite a lot of time at the Santa Barbara Zoo. It was a wonderful zoo.

Eva was full of inside information: "One day that baby gibbon lost its footing and fell into the moat," she told Veronica. "It almost mangled the zoo attendant who tried to rescue it. And Veronica, this may surprise you, but those flamingos are fed red food coloring to make their feathers pink. You see, they can't get this special shrimp that flamingos eat that naturally turn their feathers pink."

Eva knew a lot about flowers, too.

"Look at those beautiful water lilies," Veronica said one day. She wanted Eva to know she appreciated nature, too.

"Not water lilies," Eva said at once. She went over to the edge of the pond and broke off a piece of the plant. "It's an ice plant. Look!"

Veronica was amazed to see that the inside of the leaf looked like an ice crystal.

They spent hours walking along the wharf and eating ice cream. Veronica liked the way Eva said something was "way cool" when she really meant it was fantastic!

At nights and on weekends Veronica kept her father company as he worked on the big old Victorian house. They had picnics in the house and discussed Veronica's plans for the garden she would plant in the spring.

She hadn't seen Candy at all, but she was afraid to say anything. She had told her father about the earthquake dream and the pamphlet she had sent him in the letter. "But Candy probably thought it was junk mail," she said. "Besides I didn't know she was your girlfriend; I thought she was the baby-sitter!"

"She opened the letter?" her father asked. "I'm going to have to talk to her."

On the day before she had to leave, Veronica burst out, "Oh Daddy, aren't you seeing Candy anymore?"

"Nope," her father said. "No one reads my mail."

"But it was all my fault!" Veronica said.

They were sitting on the front porch of the house "taking a break."

"It wasn't your fault," her father said, "but you did me a big favor. I don't like snoops."

Veronica began telling her father about her French teacher. "She's just beautiful. Everyone calls her 'Mademoiselle.' You would really like her."

Her father laughed. "Veronica, when I need a matchmaker, I'll let you know."

"Then, of course, there's Miss Markham. . . ." Veronica looked dreamily at the overgrown garden and thought what a beautiful place it would be for a wedding. . . .

# A New Life

The next day Veronica left Santa Barbara. Her plane was delayed on the ground in Los Angeles for three hours. Veronica sat on the plane dreading the thought of going back to school.

Veronica did not get back until midnight. Her mother picked her up at the airport.

"I *knew* it wasn't a good idea for Lorenzo to put you on such a last minute flight," her mother said as they drove back to the city. "You have school tomorrow."

There was very little traffic and they made good time.

"Elaine," Veronica said, "have you decided on my punishment yet?" Nothing could come in the way of her plans for spring vacation.

"I'm still thinking about it," her mother said

absentmindedly. "Veronica, look in my bag. There's a token in there for the toll booth."

Veronica found the token and handed it to her mother.

"Well," Veronica said slowly. "You can punish me any way you like, just as long as you let me go to school tomorrow. *Please* don't keep me home. *Please* don't let that be my punishment."

Her mother was quiet.

Veronica was kept home from school, and she had a lovely day. While her mother was out at Self-Awareness Through Movement, she unpacked her suitcase. To her delight her suitcase was full of sand from East Beach. She collected it grain by grain and put it into an envelope "to treasure for the rest of my life," she told herself.

But, when Chris got home from school, she took the envelope across the hall and gave it to him. "Straight from the beach in Santa Barbara," she told him. "It's a present for taking care of Gulliver and Lady Jane Grey."

Chris seemed quite pleased with the sand. "Did you have fun in Santa Barbara?" he asked politely.

Veronica sighed. "I had such a good time, I don't even have to talk about it."

But she did anyway. She left out the part about Gulliver being an alley cat. It would not be good for Gulliver's "image," she decided.

Later that afternoon her mother took her to the hairdresser to have her hair evened out. "Who in the world gave you that haircut?" she asked. Then they went out for dinner to a small French restaurant. Veronica wondered if this were part of the punishment.

As they were eating their dessert of fresh raspberries, her mother said, "Veronica, didn't I already punish you for the piano?"

"Yes," Veronica said. "Don't you remember? No Halloween."

Her mother still seemed puzzled.

"This one is for the . . . um . . . doctor's note I wrote, the fake broken arm, making a promise to Miss Levy in bad faith, and ruining Kimberly Watson's life," Veronica explained.

"Oh," her mother said.

Her mother hadn't even remembered. Veronica had a feeling she had tricked herself! And she still had to face school again tomorrow.

Veronica had butterflies in her stomach when she stepped off the bus in front of the Maxton Academy. Hilary was standing in front of the school with a briefcase in one hand and her flowered shopping bag in the other. She ran to meet Veronica.

"Veronica!" Hilary said. "Where were you yesterday? I brought all this stuff to show you. Oh, Veronica, you did it again!"

"Did what?" Veronica asked.

Just then she saw Kimberly coming toward her. Her hair had grown out a little and it didn't look too bad.

Kimberly was furious with Veronica. "Veronica! You're the only one who hasn't seen Baby Joseph. You have to come to my house right after school today."

Veronica congratulated Kimberly on her new baby brother, but she was hoping to go to Hilary's house after school. She *had* to tell Hilary about her father. "I'll come see him tomorrow," she told Kimberly.

"Tomorrow is too late," Kimberly said. "He changes every day. You've got to see him today. Tomorrow he'll be different."

"He really is adorable," Hilary said. "We all went over yesterday and he lifted up his head and sort of bobbed it around and looked at every one of us and smiled."

"But he looked at me the longest," Amy said. She was standing behind Kimberly staring at Veronica. "You're really suntanned," she said.

"He never did that before," Kimberly said proudly. "Bobbed his head around like that."

Hilary turned to Kimberly. "Veronica and I can stop there on the way to my house," she said. "Veronica, you've got to see him. He's the friendliest baby I've ever seen."

Kimberly beamed. "I've been teaching him all sorts of things. I even sang 'Rock-a-Bye-Baby' and everyone says my voice has improved *immensely*."

Veronica felt the world was turning upside down. Kimberly seemed to have completely forgotten that, not long ago, Veronica had ruined her life.

"What's in the briefcase?" Veronica asked Hilary.

"That's the surprise," Hilary said.

Veronica followed Hilary to the top of the steps. They sat on the top step while Hilary opened the briefcase.

It was full of carbon copies of letters from kids protesting the closing of the Harding Branch of the library.

Veronica was delighted. "So those kids at the Halloween party finally wrote to the mayor!"

Hilary shook her head. "Look again."

Veronica looked at a few of the letters. Suddenly she saw a letter signed Eva Wright.

"I don't get it," she said. Then she noticed that under each signature were the words: KIDS FOR HARDING — WEST COAST CHAPTER.

"Eva and her big mouth!" Veronica said.

Hilary was smiling at her.

"Me and my big mouth, too," Veronica admitted.

At the end of the day Veronica and Hilary followed Kimberly home from school on their way to visit the new baby.

Veronica felt nervous. In all the time she had been coaching Kimberly, she had never once been invited to Kimberly's house. But she knew it was in a very elegant neighborhood. She glanced at Hilary, who was carrying the briefcase in one hand and the flowered shopping bag in the other.

154

"Look, Hilary," she said, "that briefcase looks fantastic — *way cool* — but, if I were you, I'd put all your books in the briefcase, fold up the shopping bag, and put that in the briefcase, too. It would look much nicer. . . ."

"I like it this way," Hilary said quietly.

They walked another block. Veronica felt desperate. Suddenly she burst out, "Well, then, let *me* carry the shopping bag. Just for today!"

Hilary stopped and stared at Veronica. "But I thought you didn't like the way it looks!"

"I don't care how *I* look," Veronica said. "I care how *you* look."

Hilary sighed and handed Veronica the flowered shopping bag.

"Will you two please hurry!" Kimberly shouted. "Baby Joseph is probably doing something brand new *right this minute*. We'll miss it!"

Veronica and Hilary began to run.

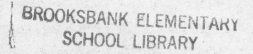

# About the Author

NANCY K. ROBINSON has written fifteen books for children, starting with a biography, *The Howling Monkeys: The Story of Ray Carpenter*, in 1973.

With *Wendy and the Bullies* in 1980 she switched to writing fiction and continues to win new fans with each new book.

*Veronica Knows Best* marks Veronica Schmidt's third appearance in a Nancy K. Robinson book, following *Just Plain Cat* (which is mostly about her neighbor, Chris) and the very popular *Veronica the Show-Off*.

In addition to writing, Ms. Robinson's special interest is photography. She has two children and lives in an apartment in New York City.